Praise for *Chrissy's Cozy Mystery Series*

This is the third installment of the Chrissy mystery series and it is my favorite! Diane continues to develop her main characters while adding amusing new characters. Autumn, Chrissy and friends have again found themselves in the middle of a mystery and use their sleuthing skills to find a murderer. You will be kept on the edge of your seat trying to solve this case! In this easy to read mystery, you will find yourself falling for the characters and the small town they live in.

—Antoinette Brickhaus, Leonardtown, MD

The plot takes several twists and turns and I suspected at least four different people of being Amy's killer and Dana's stalker. I loved how the plot unfolded and how I was kept in suspense about the killer's identity until the end. *Trick-or-Doggy Treat* is a delightful, fast-paced and engaging book well worth reading. It is a great standalone book, even if you haven't read the first two.

—Terri Chalmers, Sicklerville, NJ

Diane Wing delivers again! Return to the charming town of Knollwood, Pennsylvania, as Chrissy the furry detective returns in *Trick-or-Doggy Treat*, the exciting third adventure in the Chrissy's Cozy Mysteries series. As a passionate mystery lover, I pride myself in rapid perpetrator identification. Not this time; the tricks abound and my suspicions stayed aroused throughout the read, as Wing's diverse characters delivered a myriad of exciting distractions right through to the very end. *Trick-or-Doggy-Treat* is a delightful, satisfying cozy mystery wrapped in the rich, colorful tapestry of a Pennsylvania fall in a wonderful town. Halloween has never been this enchanting. A truly enjoyable read!"

—Maxine Ashcraft, Oakland, CA

Autumn and Chrissy are turning me into a cozy mystery fan. Chrissy once again discovers all-important clues to help solve the murder mystery. In this installment the glamour of Hollywood comes East along with an unsolved murder. How this impacts the big Halloween party creates a great opportunity to develop an exciting plot.

—Steven Cohen

This series has a calming effect on me. The author does a wonderful job of writing a page turning mystery that you can get lost in for hours. Even though it is a work of fiction, when you put the book down you feel renewed and refreshed. There is a lot of character development in this series and I enjoy seeing how the characters have developed throughout the three books. I am looking forward to seeing where the author takes the series next!

Marie McNary, *A Cozy Experience*

This was a lovely and enjoyable read! Diane Wing's descriptions are so vivid you can easily visualize and feel what is happening. Her characters are multidimensional and relatable. Looking forward to future adventures with Chrissy and Autumn!

—Judy Levin

I loved getting to know the characters better, their interactions and the motives that drive them. The dogs however need a special mention from the stoic guardian Ace to the adorable, clue sniffing Chrissy and their utter commitment to the humans that they have taken under their paw.

—*Krystyna's Reviews*

Through the relationship between Autumn and Chrissy, Wing also shows the importance of therapy animals and how much they can help those who need them. Add a sweet romance to the intrigue of the mystery and you've got a book that you won't want to put down.

—Melissa Alvarez, Intuitive, animal communicator and author of *Animal Frequency* and *Llewellyn's Little Book of Spirit Animals*

Diane Wing has created a wonderfully endearing little character in Chrissy the Shih Tzu. It really shines through that the author is a lover of animals and dogs. I can see these books quickly becoming a cherished addition to the cozy mystery genre.

—J. New, author of *The Yellow Cottage Vintage Mysteries*

If you have already met a young lady called Autumn, and her fluffy little dog, Chrissy, you'll look forward to following them with another murder investigation. If not, you are in for a pleasant surprise, and this story stands perfectly well alone. Any book worth remembering has lessons under the surface. I approve of these ones. They are mostly about human nature, and the way good people treat each other. Read, and find out what I mean.

—Bob Rich, PhD, author of *Ascending Spiral*

Trick-or-Doggy Treat

A Chrissy the Shih Tzu
Cozy Mystery

Diane Wing

Modern History Press

Ann Arbor, MI

Trick-or-Doggy Treat: A Chrissy the Shih Tzu Cozy Mystery
Copyright © 2020 by Diane Wing. All Rights Reserved.
2nd Printing – November 2020

Learn more at www.DianeWingAuthor.com

This is a work of fiction. Names, characters, places, and incidents are the products of the author's imagination or are used fictitiously. Any resemblance to actual events, locales, or persons, living or dead, is entirely coincidental. Thanks for indulging me in taking artistic license within the fictional town of Knollwood, Pennsylvania.

ISBN 978-1-61599-538-7 paperback
ISBN 978-1-61599-539-4 hardcover
ISBN 978-1-61599-540-0 eBook

Library of Congress Cataloging-in-Publication Data

Names: Wing, Diane, 1959- author.
Title: Trick-or-doggy treat : a Chrissy the Shih Tzu cozy mystery / Diane Lee Wing.
Description: 1. | Ann Arbor, MI : Modern History Press, 2020. | Series: Chrissy the Shih Tzu cozy mysteries ; 3 | Summary: "Autumn and Chrissy must solve another murder in Knollwood, PA where Hollywood starlet Dana Wood is taking refuge after learning her husband may be implicated in the death of actress Amy Davis"-- Provided by publisher.
Identifiers: LCCN 2020043618 (print) | LCCN 2020043619 (ebook) | ISBN 9781615995387 (paperback) | ISBN 9781615995394 (hardcover) | ISBN 9781615995400 (ebook)
Classification: LCC PS3623.I652 T75 2020 (print) | LCC PS3623.I652 (ebook) | DDC 813/.6--dc23
LC record available at https://lccn.loc.gov/2020043618
LC ebook record available at https://lccn.loc.gov/202004361

Published by
Modern History Press
5145 Pontiac Trail
Ann Arbor, MI

www.ModernHistoryPress.com
info@ModernHistoryPress.com
tollfree 888-761-6268
fax 734-663-6861

Distributed by Ingram (USA/CAN/AU), Bertram's Books (UK/EU)

To my husband, Frank, with love, always.

Books by Diane Wing....

Cozy Mysteries with Chrissy the Shih Tzu

Attorney-at-Paw

The Dog-Eared Diary

Trick-or-Doggy Treat

Dark Fantasy

Coven: The Scrolls of the Four Winds

Thorne Manor and other bizarre tales

Trips to the Edge

Non-fiction

The True Nature of Tarot: Your Path to Personal Empowerment

The True Nature of Energy: Transforming Anxiety into Tranquility

The Happiness Perspective: Seeing Your Life Differently

Acknowledgements

I'm so fortunate to have a diverse and devoted group of friends willing to help me with the nuances of the story. Listed in alphabetical order, these are my heroes:

My deepest gratitude goes out to Nicole Bolt Anderson, Elizabeth Morrison, Yasmine Ndassa, and Dionne Vernon for their guidance on Black and Jamaican culture. You helped me understand the subtleties in portraying my characters of color.

To my beta readers who provided heartfelt reactions and first round editing of the story: Maxine Ashcraft, Antoinette Brickhaus, and Terri "Eagle Eye" Chalmers. Thanks to Bob Rich, Ph.D. for final round editing and helpful thoughts about the story.

For those of you whose sharp eye catches any glitches that may have gotten through, please know that two editing software programs caught some errors, the humans caught others, and despite all of that some still might manage to sneak through. Please let me know if you find any so we can update the text in future editions of the book. Thank you!

A very special thank you to Chef Jacquie for providing fabulous recipes you can make at home. There are lots more on her website at www.strEATSofPhillyFoodTours.com.

Notes

Book club questions, recipes of meals from the book, and a Halloween scavenger hunt list appear at the end of the book. Enjoy!

Headlines from *The Hollywood Examiner*:

DANA WOOD BETRAYED BY HUSBAND WITH ACTOR AMY DAVIS

SUSPICIOUS DEATH OF AMY DAVIS

PRODUCER MICHAEL WILLIAMS #1 SUSPECT IN DEATH OF ACTOR

Obituary: Amy Davis (1995 -2020), Los Angeles, CA

Actor Amy Davis, 25, died Saturday, September 5, 2020, from injuries sustained in a fall while hiking.

Amy was born Dec. 14, 1995, in Reading, PA and was a Los Angeles resident for the last ten years. She appeared in several films and television productions, including *The Book Club Murders* television movie series and the supernatural film franchise *Thorne Manor I and II.*

She is survived by her aunt, Zelda Weems.

Her life celebration is at 10 a.m., September 23, at the McCall Funeral Home Chapel of Memories. Send donations in memory of Amy to The Actors Fund, 11 South Broad Street, Los Angeles, CA.

Michael had no idea how it happened. He woke up on the ground, head pounding, amidst dry bushes in a rocky terrain. Amy Davis was dead, splayed at the bottom of the cliff. The tabloids had a field day accusing him of murder. He had no reason to kill her, but the media had a way of spinning their tales to intrigue the public. Photos of him with the actor having dinner and attending an opening at a high-end art gallery in Los Angeles were splashed across the Hollywood news rags.

The walls of his wood-paneled study closed in on him as he sipped his favorite 25-year-old scotch. He squirmed in the usually comfortable wingback leather chair and reviewed his bad judgment. The small green glass shade of the desk lamp cast him in shadows.

The affair was one thing, but when the starlet turned up dead, Michael Williams knew Dana would cut him off. Not even finding a new movie deal could save him or their marriage. Award-winning actor Dana Wood didn't need him as much as he needed her, or at least as much as he needed her money.

It wasn't like he fulfilled her, and Dana didn't use her A-list acting talent to fake her feelings. He knew that her keen intuition picked up on his infidelity. He could feel her contempt from across the room whenever they were together. His public display with Amy was a mistake, but he had no desire to hide it. The underlying resentment toward Dana stemmed from his own self-loathing.

In Amy, he had found a doting admirer, amazed at his producer status and amused by his humor. His ego required her attention. He smiled easily around her and wanted to be the wonderful person she thought he was. His marital status never came up in conversation, since it was common knowledge who his wife was. Besides, relationship boundaries in the entertainment industry stretched well past the wedding vows for most.

Except for Dana. She had honor and a reputation for integrity. She was a rare person in general, let alone among the Hollywood crowd.

He could say he'd been lonely. Filming on location overseas meant that they were apart for months at a time. In her absence, his job was to find their next project and the financing to go along with it rather than a young lover. Dana always kept her end of the bargain, delivering performances that made the fans want more. He found the money; Dana brought the joy and reaped the awards.

His accomplishments all tied back to his famous wife. She enabled his success, and he'd betrayed her trust.

Despite his affection for Amy, he stayed away from her life celebration service. With the rumors of murder flying around, he thought it best for Amy's family and his own to forego attending. Her Aunt Zelda would be there, and while he had never met her in person, the stories Amy told him about her constant criticism made him wonder why Amy allowed Zelda to live with her. The woman invaded Amy's privacy and insisted on being on set with her during filming.

By all accounts, the woman was an odd duck, a throwback from the sixties with her long skirts, round sunglasses, and floppy hat. She lurked around the studio, intently watching everyone as she ate heartily from the free buffet. He guessed Amy's loyalty came from Zelda being her last remaining relative. No matter, it wasn't his problem.

Michael Williams took a gulp of scotch in the dim light of the room that used to be his sanctuary. Now it brought no safety, no motivation, no inspiration, only fear and the weight of his choices bearing down on him.

He knew that Dana's reputation for integrity, professionalism, and kindness would remain intact throughout the ordeal. The darling of the media, they admonished Michael while playing-up Dana's pain and suffering. They weren't far off the mark.

Finding out about his fling with Amy Davis and embarrassing her in public was an unforgiveable stupid move. He hoped Dana didn't divorce him. Or worse yet, never use him to produce any of her other movies. The money would go with her and life as he'd known it over. His mind searched for other vocations he qualified for and landed on salesman. The thought brought a lump into his throat.

He downed the rest of the scotch and refilled his glass. The prenuptial agreement was airtight. He'd be washed up. He needed to convince Dana to leave him with some money before they parted ways.

Nothing could make up for cheating on Dana in full public view. She had come back from Scotland greeted at the airport by reporters and horrific, front-page tabloid headlines screaming his treachery in all caps: *DANA WOOD BETRAYED BY HUSBAND WITH ACTOR AMY DAVIS*. Amy always said she wanted her name to become famous, and it had. A photo of Michael, his arm wrapped around the shoulder of the starlet who wore a severely low-cut dress, was below. A photo of Dana looking devastated next to it. Dana's photo was actually from a scene she played in a movie, but it did the job for the gossip-hungry public.

The article speculated what happened. Had Amy blackmailed Michael by threatening to tell Dana about them? Did Dana threaten her husband with divorce if he didn't get rid of Amy, so he pushed her over the cliff? Had an angry fan of Dana's hired someone to extinguish Amy's vibrancy and future and didn't have time to kill Michael, too? Or was it a jealous boyfriend of Amy's who caught her trying to further her career by dating Michael?

It was astonishing how conspiracy theories went viral and those without real information started rumors that do extensive harm to the reputations of those involved. The police found no evidence of foul play or of Michael being at fault and ruled Amy's death a hiking accident. She miscalculated her footing at the edge of an eroding trail and fell to her death. Amy's blood alcohol level confirmed that she was inebriated. Michael's was even higher, so they figured he'd passed out before she took the fall and hit his head on a rock.

The tabloid article pulled all the doubts and fears from his own mind. Was it his fault that Amy died? Was there someone hidden in the trees just off the trail, waiting for their chance to kill one or both of them?

He picked at his cuticle and took a sip of scotch, feeling its smooth heat that didn't quite reach his icy heart. It used to be easy to get the funds they needed before the name Michael Williams became synonymous with underhanded business dealings. And now cheating. It was common enough in the entertainment industry, but in his case, it added to his tarnished reputation.

The conversations about his untrustworthy business practices took place openly these days. In whispers, California investors gossiped about the death of Michael's last fling. She ended up at the bottom of a ravine in a supposed hiking accident, and suspicions raged despite no criminal charges being brought. Fixers could clean the scene to lead law enforcement astray.

Michael had not the slightest bit of memory peeking through the fog of that afternoon beyond stopping for a picnic and finishing two bottles of wine. He was very drunk at the time and woke up lying on the ground in a stupor. He could see the young actor's blonde hair splayed around her head, mixed with blood at the bottom of the ravine, but did not understand how she ended up there. He had to hike two miles back to the car to get a cell signal to call 911.

With no one wanting to work with him on the West Coast, Michael needed to fish in a different pond on the East Coast.

ೞ

Dana Wood had fought hard to rise to her current status. As a female, and a woman of color no less, she had to work ten times harder to overcome professional obstacles than men in the entertainment industry. Dana's marriage to executive producer Michael Williams got her career a little further along, but it was her veteran actor and executive friends who schooled her on how to succeed, that made her wiser than her 32 years.

Gail Armstrong, her publicist, called during the flight back from Scotland, warning Dana about the headlines involving her husband. Having her personal life displayed as entertainment for all to see went against the idea that there's no such thing as bad publicity. She only had a few hours to wrap her head around the starlet's death and her husband's cheating before facing questions from reporters.

Despite Dana's award-winning acting skills, she struggled to hide embarrassment and hurt from the persistent paparazzi lying in wait at the airport. The clicks and flashes of the cameras forever captured every reaction and micro-expression. She flooded her mind with images of Scotland and her joy working on an Oscar-quality film, giving her eyes a sparkle she did not feel.

She hurried past the chaotic din, giving brief waves and tiny smiles to the cameras of those she recognized. When Gail's slender arm waved frantically over the crowd, gold bangle bracelets bouncing up and down, Dana's chest loosened. Two massive bodyguards parted the invading hoard like the Red Sea, allowing Dana to get through. She released the breath she didn't realize she was holding. The men closed ranks behind her, blocking reporters from pursuing their target.

Gail hugged her tight, then linked elbows with Dana, rushing her toward the exit where a limo waited. Dana felt her security team on her heels. The driver opened the door, and Gail pushed Dana into the limo, scrambling in behind her. One bodyguard sat up front with the driver. The other went to retrieve their black SUV to bring up the rear. Gail had arranged for Dana's assistant to pick up her luggage at the carousel.

Both women took a few moments to catch their breath and gulp some water.

"Too bad that brouhaha wasn't about the new film," said Gail.

Dana smiled sadly and nodded. She sighed, fighting back tears.

Gail patted Dana's hand. "I got word of the situation from my friend at the police station, so it gave me time to put out press releases about your film and distance you from the situation. Your husband, or should I say soon-to-be-ex-husband, didn't notify his publicist before the press got a hold of the story."

"I should have stayed in Scotland," said Dana, sipping water and shaking her head.

"We didn't know until you were on the plane."

"I don't want to be in Los Angeles but don't want people to think I'm running away."

"Then you will love what Ken has in store for you. The timing is perfect."

Ken Blanchard was Dana Wood's manager.

Dana turned her famous hazel eyes toward Gail. "I don't know if I can stand anymore surprises right now."

Gail smiled. "I will let Ken tell you. You're going home, having a relaxing bubble bath, and going to bed."

Dana nodded in agreement.

⊂₈₂⊃

Dana entered Michael's study. Even in the dim light she was exquisite. Her dyed golden blonde hair glowed against her smooth buttery caramel brown skin. Dana Wood's large almond-shaped hazel eyes needed no makeup to enhance her beauty, but using it highlighted her cheekbones and mesmerizing gaze. He remembered a time when those gentle eyes held love for him. Now he saw only pain and the flowing tears that his actions caused.

With Michael's Welsh ancestry, he wondered what their children would have looked like if they had had any. He imagined the most beautiful offspring given Dana's extraordinary features, symmetrical face, and buttery skin tone balancing his pale complexion and blue eyes. Dana was adamant about not having children, so he would never know. She never gave a reason. It was just as well, since they had no time for children, or even a pet, and now they shared no future at all.

Even wearing jeans and a T-shirt, Dana's regal appearance came through. The way she carried herself and the flash of confidence mixed with joy in her eyes endeared her to fans and colleagues alike.

Guilt washed over him with the recognition that his folly had crushed the joy, but the confidence remained mixed with uncharacteristic coldness.

"Please start looking for another place to live." Dana said, too exhausted to say more.

Michael nodded in understanding. His imprudent actions made Dana a free agent where career, life, and love were concerned. He drained his glass as the sound of the study door slamming signaled the end of his luxurious lifestyle and his last chance at success.

⚡ **2** ⚡

Dana trudged up the winding marble staircase. She leaned heavily on the ornamental iron banister. She was bone weary from the flight, battling with the press, and conjuring the strength to banish Michael from her life once and for all.

The master bedroom at the end of the hall seemed a mile away. Clicking the door shut, she threw the deadbolt. Security experts built the elegant sanctuary with state-of-the-art locks, cameras, and security panels at Gail's insistence in response to a worrisome fan. Some fellow had sent her letters professing his love for her and assuring her he was "keeping an eye" on her. He signed it "Always, Your Protector," in a neat combination of print and script lettering.

Michael had his own suite where he and his clothes lived. He would sleep there until he found another place to live. Dana hoped that was sooner than later. She had waited one trip too many to ask him to leave. Her instincts alerted her to his affairs, and she stopped sleeping with him to avoid sexually transmitted diseases, but none of them resulted in murder until now. Even though he insisted he had no idea what happened, and the police said it was an accidental death, her gut told her otherwise.

Dana peeled off her clothes and stepped into the shower. The powerful stream of water and lavender soap washed the stress and airplane grime from her body. She washed her hair with her favorite gardenia shampoo. Free of the wigs and the weaves required of her on the movie set, it felt good to massage her scalp and release some tension.

Lotioned and powdered, she slipped into her favorite peach silk, floor-length negligee and slid between soft ivory sheets. The embroidered duvet cover pressed against her, the extra bit of weight making her feel secure.

Dana took a deep breath, glad to be back in the luxury and safety of her home. She stared at the gentle lighting that surrounded the tray ceiling above her bed and thought about how far she had come from her childhood in an affluent area of Montego Bay, Jamaica. The lush forests and grand resorts, some of which were owned by her family, gave her a taste for both luxury and nature. From beautiful clothing to educational opportunities, she moved in the wealthy circles of both business and government.

From the outside, it seemed Dana lived a charmed life, better than most in her native country. But the natural and financial abundance wasn't enough to keep dealing with her controlling parents. She met their expectations with grace. Her beauty was the envy of every woman and the desire of every man, yet Dana was a loner; she never fit it. Her perspective on life and what she wanted out of it deviated from family and schoolmates. She had a way of seeing beyond her circumstances and upbringing. Even with friends, she felt isolated.

With no one to confide in, the unexpected pregnancy made the 18-year-old Dana feel more alone than ever. An amorous evening with a United States Congressman from Virginia, Steven Hartford, visiting her family's resort put her in a precarious position. That he was Caucasian was not an issue. Her family considered conception out of wedlock, and with a married man, a shameful act, especially because of their stature in the community.

The Honorable Steven Hartford assured her he had no interest in the baby, and that his wife could not find out. He offered her money to end the pregnancy, but her heart would not consider that an option.

Torn between keeping her offspring and being cut off from the family with no means to support a child, she agreed to live with family friends in Easton, Pennsylvania for the duration of the pregnancy and the first few months of the child's life. The baby was born on Valentine's Day. She was told that the adoptive parents, who remained anonymous, were excited to get the baby. The closed adoption provided sealed records, preventing the adoptive parents from knowing who the birth mother was. Dana's despair grew as the time to give up her baby girl came closer.

After they completed the heartbreaking transaction, she realized she wanted to stay in the United States. Steven Hartford helped her get fast-tracked to citizenship on the agreement that she would not contact him again. That suited Dana perfectly.

She moved to Los Angeles, California and spent the next few years quelling her Jamaican accent to a velvety smooth California dialect. When she went home to Jamaica, she reclaimed her heritage and felt her natural idioms flow from her tongue. During those visits, her circle never discussed the pregnancy or the fate of her daughter.

She often thought of her daughter and wondered what she looked like as a teenager. What guidance were her guardians giving her? Did she wish to seek her biological parents? Would they ever reunite? Dana sent love to her child each day, along with blessings for health and happiness.

Michael's betrayal reminded her of the congressman who had cheated on his wife, and her jaw clenched. Dana's humiliation made her feel powerless, reminding her of when she had to give up her child. She'd been searching for ways to get her power back, and part of her healing journey included banishing Michael from her life.

She clicked the television remote control and was asleep five minutes after she started watching a show about people in search of an island to buy.

＊ **3** ＊

Ken Blanchard moved a miniature rake through a desktop Japanese sand garden as he spoke on his headset. His therapist said it would keep him calm. He didn't think it worked.

"Yes, please send her in."

Dana entered his office. Her smooth caramel skin glowed in the streaming sunlight.

"You're looking well, all things considered," said Ken, pretend-kissing her on each cheek and waving her over to the comfortable sitting area overlooking downtown Los Angeles.

Ken had been Dana's manager for the last ten years. He also represented other A-listers, who Dana counted as pleasant acquaintances. She wasn't sure there were any genuine friendships in Hollywood, only beneficial alliances.

"Gail is taking care of the PR nightmare, but I'm not sure I want to stick around here while Michael moves out and the press has fun speculating about what happened."

"Then I have good news for you. Albert Holton is launching a new project."

"I love working with Albert!"

"And he feels the same about you. He's requested you as the leading lady for *Dark Hollow Road*. It's a cross between mystery and fantasy where a grieving sister searches for her brother on a road notorious for missing persons."

"It doesn't sound like my usual genre."

She preferred the drama films she was known for, with meaty characters that transformed over the course of the story. She won Academy Awards and People's Choice Awards for her leading and supporting roles.

"No, but it introduces you to a new, younger audience. Albert has taken several A-listers and put them in unconventional roles with huge box office success."

She went quiet, considering this information.

"Most importantly, the investors are excited to work with the likes of Dana Wood. Best of all, they're filming in New Hope, Pennsylvania. You can escape and enjoy the fall colors."

That was only an hour from Easton, where she stayed during her pregnancy. The family she stayed with had gone back to Jamaica, but she was familiar with the area. Dana wanted to get away from the local gossip, and this might be the perfect solution since she enjoyed the scenery there.

Another appealing aspect was that Michael had no part in producing the film. Dana had not spoken to him in days. He left her a note in the kitchen saying he'd be out of the house within the month.

"I know you hate the rumor mill, but the situation with Michael could only boost interest in the film. It's free press."

Yes, to everyone other than Dana Wood.

"When do I leave?"

≉ 4 ≉

The Peabody Mansion Halloween Extravaganza was only two weeks away. Workers toiled in the basement to have the shops and bowling alley ready for the hundreds of locals and tourists Autumn Clarke hoped would attend. The fire marshal ordered an emergency exit at the far end of the basement, and it was being installed. They needed to keep a close eye on the flow of traffic since the cavernous space had a limit of one hundred fifty patrons. The overflow could enjoy festivities on the main level and in the outdoor spaces.

The posters around town promised grand Halloween fun, including a costume contest, a hay bale maze, and a pumpkin carving event. The ticket price benefitted the local animal shelter.

Chrissy, a sweet little Shih Tzu with long flowing hair, trotted through the entry foyer of the grand stone mansion. Autumn inherited it, along with a fortune, from the Peabody clan, a family she never knew she had until recently, but Chrissy was the actual princess of the castle.

Autumn was excited to share the space with the community. Chrissy's tail bounced and her hips swayed as she charmed workers who bent down to pet her luxurious hair. Autumn replaced Chrissy's signature pink ribbons with black and orange bows to mark the upcoming holiday.

Autumn stood behind the reception desk, taking notes while cradling the phone between her shoulder and her ear. Chrissy joined her in search of her comfy pink and white bed tucked under the desk. As social as she could be, Chrissy also needed a place to escape from the commotion and be near her mommy. Autumn petted the cottony soft head before going back to her call. Chrissy stepped onto the fuzzy cushion, turned around a few times, and then settled in with her chin on the raised edge of the doggy bed, letting out a deep sigh.

"That would be great, Elizabeth. I'm looking forward to seeing you this afternoon for a walk-through."

Autumn hung up the phone and bent down to pet Chrissy.

"I know it's been noisy here. You're so good."

Chrissy looked up adoringly at Autumn, then settled back in. She had been Autumn's saving grace as she dealt with PTSD from the car accident that killed her parents. Chrissy had lost her daddy to murder,

13

and as destiny would have it, Autumn found her at the shelter and they immediately had a strong connection. They pretty much rescued each other. Now that Autumn's symptoms were under control, what remained between them was unconditional love.

The desk phone rang. Autumn answered with her standard chipper greeting.

"Peabody Mansion Bed and Breakfast. This is Autumn. How may I help you?"

"Hi, Autumn. I'm Cheryl Anderson from Albert Holton's office."

Autumn paused. She took a deep breath.

"You mean Albert Holton, the director?" Autumn's heart fluttered. His movies were some of her favorites.

"That's the one," Cheryl said with a smile in her voice.

"What can I do for you?" Autumn couldn't control her excitement.

"I found your website, and the place is perfect. We know that your B&B isn't open to the public just yet. Mr. Holton wondered if you could make an exception for one of his actors coming in from the West Coast."

Banging and sawing noises came wafting up from the basement.

"We have some construction going on for about another week. If that's okay, I'm happy to accommodate your actor."

"Great! She'll be flying in on Sunday."

It was Monday, giving Autumn plenty of time to get the room ready.

"We'll complete most of the noisy activities by then. I'll ready the largest suite we have."

"Thank you so much for helping us out."

"My pleasure. What is the guest's name?" Autumn poised the pen over the record book.

"Dana Wood."

The pen skidded and adrenaline made Autumn's hand shake.

"Dana Wood! We're honored to have her as our very first guest! Please let me know if there are any special accommodations she requires."

"For someone so famous, she's surprisingly low maintenance."

Autumn and Cheryl shared a laugh.

"Fair warning: it's hard to ensure Ms. Wood's privacy in a small town, especially since we're hosting a Halloween event."

"That's fine. They're filming in New Hope, so people will know she's here no matter what you do. And Ms. Wood loves Halloween, so that's a bonus."

"How exciting! We'll make her stay here a pleasant one."

"Thank you."

Cheryl gave Autumn her email address to send the invoice.

"By the way, I have nine more rooms I can ready for any others who may need them. I'll keep it to those involved with the production, so they'll have the place to themselves."

"Good to know. The other actors and crew members are fairly local, but Mr. Holton has added out-of-towners now and again."

No sooner had they hung up, Autumn grabbed her cellphone and was speed-dialing her fiancé, Detective Ray Reed.

"Hey, Pumpkin. How are the renovations going?"

"Right on schedule. But that's not why I'm calling. First, promise me you won't mention this. I'm sharing the information on a need-to-know basis."

"Haven't I proven I can keep a secret after the whole Peabody heritage incident?"

"Of course."

"Well?"

"Guess who is going to be our first guest?"

"You mean in June?"

"Nope, it's a special request for this Sunday."

"Way ahead of schedule. Give me a hint."

"Who do you always say is the most beautiful woman, other than me?"

"Dana Wood?"

"Yep!" Autumn was breathless saying it out loud. "They're shooting a film in New Hope, and she needs a place to stay."

"Wow! That's exciting."

"I wanted you to be the first to know. You're welcome to meet her, as long as you behave yourself."

"I can't imagine being with anyone but you."

Autumn laughed. "Good answer. Let's keep it that way."

"I'm sure she has better prospects than the likes of me."

"Once she meets you, she'll compare all Hollywood leading men to you." Autumn sincerely believed that Ray was the best man in the world. "If we need extra protection for her, can you arrange that?"

"My pleasure. I'm sure Adam would jump at the chance. He's a big fan."

"Sounds good. Now I have to call Lisa to arrange food. See you later?"

"Ace and I will be there around dinnertime. I want to check the progress in the basement."

They disconnected the call. Autumn pounded her cellphone and got Lisa Coleman on the line. Not only was she Autumn's neighbor and friend, but she served the best breakfast and lunch in the area.

"Coleman's Kitchen!" said Lisa. Her voice sounded rushed, the din of a full café in the background.

"Hey, Lisa."

"Autumn! Sorry, I didn't look at the caller ID. What's up? I have a packed house. Let me call you after the morning breakfast rush."

"Sounds good."

Autumn hung up, disappointed that she didn't get to tell her big news to Lisa, but thrilled that Lisa's business was succeeding. Her news was so special that it was best savored and shared when Lisa could enjoy the moment with her.

Banging and the sound of a squeaky wheel alerted Chrissy to some new activity. She jumped from her nest and trotted over to the sound. Kim Stokes, the housekeeper, came around the corner pushing her noisy cart. Chrissy wagged her tail, and Kim stopped to pet her.

Autumn grabbed a can of lubricant from under the desk and sprayed the wheel. Moving it back and forth to ensure they defeated the squeak.

"Thanks," said Kim, brightly. "That noise was driving me crazy."

"You're welcome." Autumn shook the can. "This comes in handy around here. I keep it under the desk in case you need it again."

"Good to know."

Kim came to work for the B&B when Autumn put an ad in the local paper and hung posters at the supermarket and the library. Kim was one of five candidates that responded. Autumn chose her for her cheerful disposition and her potential for promotion for front desk duties. At 25, Kim's big blue eyes and dark brown bobbed hair gave a friendly, approachable, and mature air.

"Kim, we're having a very special guest coming on Sunday, and may have some others, so please make sure the upstairs bedrooms and bathrooms are guest ready. Ray and I will stay here, too."

"I thought we weren't opening until June. Just cleaning up the construction dust has been challenging."

"Let's seal the rooms with plastic after you work your magic."

"And the bedding?"

"New sheets and quilts are called for. Let me work on that."

"Okay."

"I know, it's hard keeping up. I appreciate the outstanding job you're doing."

Kim smiled and pushed the cart into the elevator. Autumn had it installed last week. It was one of her more worthwhile investments.

Autumn punched in Beatrice Peabody's number. Autumn's relationship with her cousin started out contentious, but had smoothed since they first met. Including Bea on projects at the mansion helped to make her feel important and wanted. It was nice having a family member to call on. She picked up on the first ring.

"Hi, Bea."

"Hi, Autumn." Bea's voice was still a little scratchy from injuries sustained while managing fallout from their last case.

"Are you busy right now? I was wondering if you could help me with something."

"I'm open the rest of the day."

"Great! I need someone who has good taste in décor."

"Then you called the right number." Autumn heard the pride well in her rough voice.

"Turns out we're having unexpected guests at the mansion starting this weekend, and I need new bedding for all the rooms. Could you please go to the store and pick out ten comforter sets and double that number in matching sheet sets?"

"Definitely! I'll take Jasper with me to help load the SUV. I know you painted the upstairs. Any color changes I should know about? And I want to confirm bed sizes."

Jasper Wiggins formerly worked for Beatrice's brother Oxnard. After Oxnard died, Jasper agreed to stay on as house manager for Beatrice. Autumn was glad the two had become friendly.

They exchanged information and decided that besides being gender neutral, the blankets should also be durable and washable. Autumn would ask Kim to launder the old bedding. The delicate family heirlooms would go into the homes of Bea and Autumn.

"You're the best," ended Autumn.

"See you later," Bea said with more enthusiasm than Autumn had heard in her voice in a while.

She trusted Bea's taste and could check-off another task from her list, but more importantly, she enjoyed making Bea feel needed and valued.

The heavy front door swung open and thick, well-worn boots pounded dirt onto the outdoor welcome mat. Knollwood's jack-of-all-trades, Ward Everly, stepped inside and squatted down to pet one of his biggest fans. He was handsome in a rough sort of way, with his muscles bulging under his T-shirt and red flannel jacket. The faded jeans added to the unassuming presence of the forty-something man known for his surprising talents revealed only when a customer needed it most, Chrissy's tail swished in rapid movement, happy to see the man who always had a jerky treat at the ready.

"I know what you want," he said, reaching into his pocket. He broke off a bite-sized piece of the snack so that Chrissy's little mouth could handle it. She walked away with her prize to eat safely behind the desk.

"Hey, Ward. How are you doing?"

"Come to show you the design."

He walked over to the reception desk and unrolled a scroll he'd made from taping multiple pieces of copy paper together. Autumn noticed precise measurements for lengths, widths, and elevations.

"Wow, this looks complicated."

"You don't want an easy hay bale maze for your guests, now do ya?"

Ward's gift for designing a hay bale maze was one of those surprise skills discovered when he'd overheard Autumn in the supermarket telling someone about her Halloween plans.

"It will fit right into the clearing over to the side of the house. I'll make a path to the maze. Uplighting will make the maze and trees look eerie. Maybe put some haunted house sounds here and there triggered as people navigate the maze."

"This is genius! Better than anything I envisioned."

Ward's sun-wrinkled face deepened with a satisfied smile.

"I'll get started, then." He rolled up his design and moved toward the door. Chrissy came running from behind the desk and licked her lips. "Okay, one more." He broke off another piece and handed it to Chrissy. She wagged her thanks and went back to her hiding place. Ward waved and left.

Autumn watched him go, realizing that she knew very little about him. He showed up when needed and then disappeared until the next time she had an out-of-the-ordinary request.

The phone rang, and Autumn answered.

"Peabody B&B. How can I help you?"

"Help is the million-dollar word," said Lisa Coleman.

"People love eating at your place. Have gratitude and help will arrive." Autumn used this philosophy a great deal. It had always worked in her life.

"I know. I know."

"So, I need to add to your workload."

Lisa laughed.

"Of course! Any chance you can send Kim over here to help?"

Autumn smiled.

"She has her hands full here. I'll bet if you posted a sign in your window or put flyers at the supermarket and library, you'd get plenty of applicants."

"Good idea. I'll do that today."

"Okay, so I'm going to need your catering expertise."

"Right, for the Halloween Extravaganza."

"And to provide breakfast for my very first guest."

"I thought you're not officially open until June."

"Plans change. Gotta roll with it." Autumn's news was too good to blurt out all at once.

"So for one guest, you want me to come there and cook breakfast?"

"Yep. It would probably have to be early. Before you open for your customers."

"Seriously? Are you planning to get an in-house chef at some point?" Lisa was already pushing her energy to the limit. A multi-vitamin may be in order.

"You're the only one I'd trust with this particular job. A week from today."

"That gives me time to work my schedule around it."

"Great! I'm sure Dana Wood will appreciate it."

"The famous actor? Now you're pulling my leg."

"Not at all. She's my first guest!" Autumn was breathless with excitement.

"That's amazing! You have the most unbelievable luck."

"I'll say. She's coming here to film a movie, and the director's assistant found the Peabody B&B online, and Dana is flying in on Sunday."

"She'll probably want dinner. I can accommodate that, too!"

Autumn grinned at Lisa's enthusiasm.

"You sure you're not too busy?"

"Wise guy. Let's talk later. Another group of customers just came in."

After the call, they hung up. Autumn clapped and jumped up and down, drawing out Chrissy to see what was going on. Autumn lifted her up and kissed her. If she gave Dana Wood an exceptional experience, the B&B would succeed beyond her dearest dreams. The business' reputation depended on it. There was a chance that things could go terribly wrong. Autumn mentally drew a red circle with a line through it across the negative thought and refocused on Chrissy.

"Wait until Dana meets you!" Autumn danced around the foyer with Chrissy snuggled against her.

⚡ 5 ⚡

Elizabeth Johnson grabbed her drawings and put them in a yellow file folder, then tucked it inside her ample briefcase, along with samples of the decorations she had planned for the Peabody Mansion. The stone facade and arched doorways inspired her, and the Halloween season got her creative juices flowing.

The owner of the B&B was the type of client she desired. When asked how she found her business, Autumn replied that she checked the list of local minority-owned businesses and liked the description of how Elizabeth works. Specifically, the part about "building a creative partnership with her clients" appealed to Autumn.

She threw on a rusty orange fringed sweater that picked up the warm tones in her brown skin. The sweater went well with her twisted double pom-pom hairstyle that friends said made her look "artsy and cute." At thirty-two years old, she liked the idea of cute, the look Elizabeth equated with youthful. Elizabeth went out the door. She preferred to be a few minutes early for her appointments and leaving now would get her to the job site about 15 minutes early.

The tree-lined street led her to the driveway of the Peabody Museum. The house was a bit farther down the street, but Elizabeth wanted to walk the path that patrons of the Halloween Extravaganza would take. It gave her ideas on the experience she wanted them to have from the moment they parked their vehicles to the point they entered the mansion.

She secured the shoulder strap of her briefcase and grabbed her clipboard, making notes about the parking lot, along with ideas on decorating the entry to the museum as an add-on service. Elizabeth made her way up the street. Dense woods shaded the road and gave her ideas for scarecrows, pumpkins, and twinkle lights randomly placed along this stretch of trees. In daylight, it would offer a fun preview of what was to come. In the evening, the décor would give an eerie effect to put visitors in a Halloween mood.

Elizabeth's mother had chastised her as a child for being so enamored by Halloween. She decorated her bedroom with mummies, werewolves, ghosts, and vampires, all glowing in the Blacklight that replaced the 70-watt soft light bulb her mother had chosen. She

21

remembered her mother saying, "How can you sleep in here?" Elizabeth just laughed.

She missed her mother, who had passed away last year from cancer. She made a monumental effort to replace the sadness of the year in treatment with amusing things her mother used to do and say. This helped manage the grief to a point. That and staying busy with work.

The driveway to the mansion was wide, announced by a large carved wood sign that said Peabody Mansion Bed & Breakfast, and a small hanging sign below it that said booking for June 2021. It seemed so far in the future, but the way time flew, it was practically around the corner.

Elizabeth understood about planning in advance. Her entire business revolved around the major holidays, birthdays, and anniversaries, some of which booked years in advance. Word-of-mouth was her best marketing strategy, and her clients booked her year after year. Keeping meticulous records of past themes was essential to provide her customers with new and exciting décor.

Her art degree from the Tyler School of Art at Temple University gave her the credentials and the focus for a thriving business. The dream of expanding required hiring a full-time staff, or at the very least one other person.

The ideas flooded onto the clipboard as she mounted the stone steps, making one last note before entering the grand foyer. A woman danced with a fluffy dog in the middle of the room. She spun around and, seeing Elizabeth, stopped moving and started laughing.

"Hello. Just having a solitary celebration with Chrissy. I'm Autumn." She held out her right hand and held onto Chrissy with her left.

Elizabeth smiled and shook her hand. "I'm Elizabeth Johnson. What a wonderful way to celebrate whatever it is you're happy about." She stroked Chrissy's back. "Hello, Chrissy."

Chrissy gazed at Elizabeth and wagged her tail. Autumn put her down.

"Let's go in the living room by way of the kitchen." She looked at Chrissy. "Sorry, sweetheart, you're not allowed in here."

Chrissy sat in the hallway next to the kitchen door while Autumn closed the door. She was used to this area, since it led to the back door where her leash and harness hung on a hook. Chrissy's water and food bowls and snack plate were tucked into a nook.

Elizabeth followed Autumn into a massive stainless steel and white subway tile kitchen.

"Tea, coffee, or hot chocolate?"

"Any herbal tea?"

Autumn showed her the selection.

"After 12 noon I only drink herbal," said Autumn.

Elizabeth selected mint. Autumn chose chamomile with lavender. They spooned honey in before Autumn poured boiling water into each of their mugs. She brought a bowl of fresh water for Chrissy and placed it in the puppy nook. Chrissy drank delicately before accompanying her mommy and their guest into the living room.

The Palladian window took up most of the wall and had a comfy window seat. Elizabeth hoped she'd get to spend some time there at some point, but it wasn't practical to show Autumn drawings and samples, so she sat next to Autumn on the couch and unloaded her briefcase onto the wooden coffee table. Chrissy jumped up and snuggled between the two women.

"I like your bows, little girl," Elizabeth said to Chrissy. Then to Autumn, "This place is amazing," she said, looking at the carved ceiling and the beautiful furnishings. "My favorite is the window seat."

"Mine, too. I have a smaller one in my house, and it's the best place to read a book and let Chrissy get a little sun."

"I'm excited about this project. Thanks for inviting me to give you a proposal."

"Sure. From the looks of the portfolio on your website, I think your style is perfect for the feeling I'm trying to create. Not too scary, but festive and seasonal. Many locals will be here, so be sure to leave lots of business cards around."

"I appreciate that, but I haven't gotten the job yet."

"It feels like we're on the same wavelength already." Autumn smiled and took a sip of tea. "And Chrissy seems to like you. She sat between us. If she sat on the other side of me, that's her signal to keep away from someone."

"Got it. Thanks for the seal of approval, Chrissy." Elizabeth gently stroked her, then turned back to the table.

"I parked at the museum and made a good collection of notes for the venue approach. Am I correct that visitors will park there and walk to the main building?"

"Yes."

"Perfect!" Elizabeth walked Autumn through her thoughts, then asked, "Did you also want some decorations around the museum entrance?"

"I was thinking cornstalks and pumpkins, but I'm not the decorator. Just because I have an idea doesn't mean that's what we need to go with. *Creative partners*, right?"

Elizabeth liked the way Autumn worked and felt comfortable sitting there with the two of them. Some clients made her feel nervous, as if the job wasn't done to their exact specifications, they would give her a critical review.

"Exactly. But I can picture that and add some orange twinkle lights."

"Love it. I'd also like us to go up in the attic and see if there is anything we can use. I've actually never been up there, so if you're game, we can explore it together."

"I'm all for an adventure!" Elizabeth was getting more excited about this job. She used to love going in her grandmother's attic and perusing all the treasures.

"One more idea. My best friend, Stephanie, teaches fifth grade at Knollwood Elementary. Any chance you'd consider giving a pumpkin carving class and incorporating their creations into the design?"

"That's a great idea."

"Wonderful. They'll likely be here with their parents and can point out their work."

Elizabeth showed her some drawings and samples she'd brought with her. Autumn nodded and approved the drawings.

"Let's agree that these represent the foundation of the project, but we'll stay flexible in case some unforeseen circumstance comes up."

"Yes, of course."

"Finally, Ward Everly is building a hay bale maze in the clearing. Are you able to work with him to give it your added touches?"

"Sure. I haven't worked with him before, but he has an excellent reputation. I'm sure we'll get along fine."

"Welcome aboard," said Autumn.

Elizabeth grinned from ear to ear, something she hadn't done since her mom passed away. They made a date to explore the attic on Wednesday and said their farewells.

≈ 6 ≈

Autumn's best friend, Stephanie Douglas, and her boyfriend, local police officer Adam Miller, walked hand in hand through the trails of the Peabody Mansion. Autumn and the local landscaping company did a beautiful job creating meandering pathways on her thirty acres with surprises around each bend. Stephanie especially liked the pond with a bench dedicated in loving memory to Autumn's parents, Stella and George Clarke, who were killed in a car accident. They would have loved sitting there gazing at the ducks and listening to the birds.

Statues of fairies, gargoyles, buddhas, and pagodas stood throughout the woods, some near the path and others amidst the shadowy areas beneath old-growth trees. Each one had spaces to secure battery-operated tea lights, giving the trail a mystical appearance at night. Curved tree benches hugged the maples and oaks. Scattered along the trail, mismatched seating shaped like butterflies, mushrooms, and traditional garden benches offered visitors a variety of places to sit and reflect.

"This is going to look even more amazing decorated for Halloween," said Adam.

"I wonder where she's putting the graveyard," Stephanie added, with a grin.

Both of them loved Halloween. Last year they'd spent Halloween alone. This year, they had each other and an extensive Halloween season agenda with a list of movies, candy to eat and to give out, candy corn and all, pumpkin flavored food and beverages, butternut squash soup, and events like the spooky hayride and haunted house at Appleworth's Farm. The list included Autumn's Halloween Extravaganza, which neither of them would miss for the world. It was the first proper party at the mansion. They spent hours brainstorming costume ideas, but hadn't decided on one yet.

They emerged from the shaded trail just as Autumn and Chrissy came outside.

"Hey, you guys! It's a beautiful day to enjoy the trails," said Autumn.

"They came out better than what you had described," Stephanie replied.

"Definitely," Adam chimed in.

25

"I'm glad you're here. I need to talk to both of you. Do you have a few minutes?"

Chrissy trotted over to them, tail wagging. They both reached down to pet her.

"Whatever you need," said Stephanie, her curiosity piqued.

"I've just hired Elizabeth Johnson to decorate for the party." Autumn handed Stephanie her card. "I asked her to partner with you and your fifth graders to carve pumpkins to use in the décor."

"My kids would love that! I even know of a kid-safe pumpkin carving kit we can use. I'll give her a call."

"I know the school budget is tight, so let me know how much money you need to get them."

"Deal!" Stephanie's mind was lit with ideas on how to structure the pumpkin carving lesson.

"Adam, I'm going to need some extra security."

"Yeah, Ray already arranged for some of our guys to be around during the Extravaganza."

"I'm talking about before and after the party. We're having a very special first guest here at the inn."

Adam and Stephanie looked at each other.

"Sounds serious. Is a dignitary coming or something?" Adam chuckled.

"Even better," Autumn teased.

"Will you tell us already?" Stephanie urged.

"Have you ever heard of Dana Wood?"

"What?!" Stephanie clutched her heart and took a few steps back.

"Wow… wow… uh… wow," stammered Adam.

"She's filming a movie in New Hope, and the director wants her to stay here!" Autumn clapped her hands together.

"Sure, I'll guard her! Or whatever she needs."

"Oh, really?" Stephanie tapped her foot on the ground. "How about all of our Halloween plans? What about me? I'm not sure I want you alone with that much gorgeousness."

Autumn laughed. "I told Ray the same thing."

"I'm always available for a damsel in distress," Adam taunted them.

"I'm feeling distressed right now. Maybe she has her own bodyguard," Stephanie said, hope rising in her voice.

"I just want to be prepared in case she needs protection," said Autumn. "She'll be here on Sunday. We'll know more then."

"I'm in," said Adam.

"Me too," Stephanie offered. "I can also be here in the evening after school to keep you company." She patted his cheek.

"Well, that's mighty thoughtful of you, ma'am," said Adam in a fake accent and tipping his hat.

Stephanie smacked him lightly on the arm.

"Thanks, guys. I've got lots to do, so I'll talk to you later." Autumn waved as she and Chrissy walked back into the mansion.

"This is so exciting! I can't wait to meet her!" said Stephanie.

"You know you have nothing to worry about, right Steph?" said Adam.

Stephanie hugged him. "Right."

≉ 7 ≉

Gail Armstrong paced in front of the television in her office. The entertainment channels carried the news of Amy Davis' death and the involvement of Michael Williams. Amy's aunt, Zelda Weems, loved the attention and agreed to interviews on every station. She painted a picture of the angelic Amy gallivanting with that evil producer, Michael. You could almost see the halo over Amy's head in the photos the press used to illustrate the story. If they could have drawn horns on Michael, they would have.

Using the gossip-fixers who occupied the shadows of Hollywood had not quelled the speculation and excitement of a story closely associated with Dana Wood. The expectations for Dana to file for divorce from Michael were high. That's how the stories unfolded. Murder. Betrayal. Divorce.

The stories followed a similar format, with Dana Wood as the ultimate victim, betrayed by her husband and his younger girlfriend. While the initial investigation determined accidental death, Zelda, the public, and the press had opinions of their own. In their minds, Michael was guilty, and how could he do this to their beloved Dana.

Gail worked hard to make Dana's role in the upcoming Albert Holton film the primary story, but knew the juicier stuff had to run its course.

Gail worried about Dana's mental state as she dealt with all of this and how it would affect her role in the new movie. She didn't like Dana flying across the country by herself to ruminate about the scandal and deal with reporters on her own. As her publicist, Gail concerned herself with how the public viewed Dana, and as her friend, she also cared about how the woman herself was dealing with the situation. Fame was a double-edged sword for Dana. It brought wealth and personal difficulties in equal measure. She was a private person, loving her work, but keeping much of her personal life secret, even from Gail.

Gail's protective instincts kicked in. She called Albert Holton's assistant, Cheryl, to arrange for transportation throughout Gail's stay and asked her to book another room at The Peabody Mansion Bed & Breakfast. Her own assistant, Andrea, booked a first-class seat next to Dana on the flight to Philadelphia International Airport.

⚞ **8** ⚟

Ray and Ace walked into the mansion. The sound of hammering had quieted for the evening. Ace went up to Chrissy, and they touched noses. Autumn looked up from her work and smiled. Her loving gaze was the best part of his day.

"How's it going?" Ray asked and kissed her.

"Much better now that it's quiet. Got a lot done today." She listed all the work she scheduled and the pending projects. "Elizabeth and I are going up in the attic to see what we can use for the festivities."

"Sounds fun. Wish I could join you. Wednesday is a busy day."

"What's going on?"

"There's an opening for Lieutenant, and my interview is on Wednesday afternoon."

"That's wonderful news!"

"It's more of a management role, so I'm hoping for more regular hours. It depends on what's going on."

"I'm sure you'll get it, if that's what you really want."

"My work in the community gives me an edge over the other applicants and having relationships with city officials also helps. Part of the job is setting schedules and hiring."

"Good. I'll need you and/or Adam to help me transport Dana Wood to the movie set and back."

"How about from the airport?"

"They already hired a limousine service for that."

"That's fine. We'll work it out."

"Stephanie wants to go, too. She doesn't want Adam alone with Dana."

"But you'll trust me to go alone?"

"If I can't trust you, then we shouldn't get married." Autumn spun the engagement ring on her finger.

"True."

The door slammed open and in walked Beatrice Peabody with her house manager, Jasper Wiggins, loaded down with giant bags. If they fell, they'd have a soft landing. Ray ran over to help, and Autumn went out to the car to unload the rest.

"What's all this?" Ray asked.

"The fresh and fabulous look for the guest rooms," said Bea.

Autumn stumbled in with two more bags of comforters and pillows. She opened one of them.

"How beautiful! The pattern and the colors are lovely."

Bea puffed up with pride.

"Jasper helped."

"I did. It was quite an excursion."

Autumn peeked in the rest of the bags, equally satisfied with everything Bea chose.

"I'm sure Dana Wood is going to love this one," Autumn said as she pulled out a luxurious quilt with an acanthus-leaf design in sage and gray.

"That's my favorite, too, I… what? Who?" said Beatrice.

"Dana Wood. Didn't you say she's in one of your favorite movies?" said Autumn, continuing to admire the quilt.

"What does she have to do with…? Are you kidding? She's the unexpected guest coming on Sunday?" Beatrice plopped down on the blue velvet foyer sofa.

Autumn smiled. "I wanted to surprise you."

"That's an understatement!" Beatrice fanned herself with her hand.

Chrissy ran over to her and pushed her head against Beatrice's leg.

"I'm okay, little one."

"I just got word that her publicist is also staying."

Jasper commented, "Business is picking up, and you're not even open."

"I had Kim launder the heirloom bedding. It's folded and bagged in the den. We could use them in our own homes. Take your pick."

Ray knew the family heirlooms were especially important to Beatrice. He also knew that Autumn was fine giving Bea whatever she wanted. After all, it had been her family longer than it had been Autumn's. Her generous spirit and open heart made him love her even more.

଒ஐ

Beatrice found the pile of bedding that had been in her family for generations. Embroidery, crocheted edges, beadwork, all handmade by aunts, grandmothers, and mothers. These were the real treasures of their family fortune. She pulled open the carefully folded bedspread. She remembered this being on her mother's bed. She'd stand next to it and trace the pattern with her finger, hoping she would have the talent to make something just as beautiful one day. Turned out she didn't have the necessary skill, but she deeply appreciated the abilities of those who did.

Bea chose one for her bedroom, one for the guest room, and one for Jasper's room. She thought about how she had misjudged Autumn when they'd first met. She was fair, kind, and more compassionate than her own brother and parents had been to her. From making sure she continued to serve on the Peabody Foundation board to including her in activities at the inn and personal life, it was apparent that Autumn's parents raised her to care about others.

Without friends, without family, Bea's loneliness would have consumed her. Autumn seemed to sense that Bea needed care and inclusion despite her outwardly gruff personality. Even after the shabby way she'd treated Autumn, the woman opened her heart and gave Beatrice a full life. People tended to avoid her before Autumn came along. Over the last few months, she visibly softened, inside and out. More local folks felt comfortable approaching her now. Even the staff at the museum seemed happy to see her. As others accepted her, she could accept herself, and it showed.

CG80

By the time Beatrice emerged from the den, Ray was downstairs checking on the construction progress and Ace and Chrissy were playing with a ball in the living room. Autumn kept some of Chrissy's toys at the mansion to give her something to do while Autumn worked. Jasper had taken the purchases to the second floor, stored them in one of the bedrooms, and returned to his post in the foyer.

Jasper saw Beatrice carrying the bedding and rushed to assist.

"I chose this one for your bed, Jasper."

His eyebrows went up as she handed him the coverlet with an oak tree embroidered on it.

"This is quite an honor. Thank you." He received it with reverence.

"That looks perfect for him, Bea," Autumn said, admiring her choice. "What about choosing a couple to put in the Peabody Museum? Maybe you can write a story to go with them."

"I'd love that," Bea's eyes lit up.

"I only want one, so I'll leave it to you to determine which one is meant for me."

"I already know. It's the one with the most beads and embroidery making intricate patterns of swirls."

"I love that one! You're really good at this. Would you mind showing Kim which bedding goes where?"

"I'd be delighted," Bea said.

"When was the last time you were in the attic, Bea?"

"Around twenty years ago. Why?"

"I'm going up there tomorrow with Elizabeth, the holiday decorator, to see if there are any Halloween-type items we can use at the Extravaganza. Want to join us and give us a family history lesson?"

"Sure."

"She'll be here around one o'clock."

"See you then!"

Chrissy barked a farewell.

Ray emerged from the basement.

"Everything is progressing according to plan. Maybe even sooner than planned. Just the clean-up, and the vendors can move their stuff in by Friday."

"Is the emergency exit finished?"

"Yep, signage and emergency bar completed."

Autumn checked another item off of her to-do list.

⸗ 9 ⸗

Zelda Weems walked from room to room in Amy Davis' former home. Amy paid the rent through November, so Zelda had two months to figure out where she'd live. The television stations paid for her interviews. Not a lot, but enough to stay fed.

Amy told her aunt she was the sole beneficiary of her possessions and money, so Zelda searched Amy's files for a will. She made calls to Amy's agent and attorney to see if they knew about any legal documents with Zelda's name on them. She expected the death certificate any day now, which she'd take to the bank and transfer Amy's accounts into her own name.

Zelda planned to sell most of the objects and clothing Amy accumulated. She hoped they had an elevated value with Amy being dead and all. Zelda wasted no time and inventoried the house room by room, including Amy's clothes. Designed for Amy's slender, long-waisted and large chested body, her expensive clothing didn't fit Zelda's bulging frame. She tried squeezing herself into a casual dress, but got stuck partway in. After wrestling out of it, Zelda threw it on the bed and added it to the giveaway pile. The sale list was for Amy's expensive gowns and exclusive designer pieces.

Born to Zelda's sister, Anna, Amy was always a little tart, her primary talent shared widely among her male classmates. Zelda positioned herself as Amy's confidant and truest friend, so when Zelda was the last remaining family member, Amy clung to her. Zelda knew that Amy's lifestyle would be her undoing. Lots of jealous girlfriends had it out for Amy. And some male friends, too, those vying for her attention and thwarted with the amorous prowess of another suitor. Zelda had these sinful tidbits and more in a notebook awaiting a best-selling publication. No embellishment needed.

But the one thing that Zelda had yet to reveal was a creepy letter from an unknown fan sent to Amy when she'd first started her relationship with Michael, admonishing her for dating a married man. It reminded her of how her own father had preached about being faithful as he was cheating on her mother. The letter detailed how Dana Wood was a national treasure, and Amy's treachery deserved harsh punishment. Whoever the author was, they knew about the affair before the rumors about Amy and Michael hit the Hollywood grapevine. The typed message revealed nothing of the gender of the writer, and the postmark showed they mailed it from La Jolla.

At Amy's funeral, Zelda glimpsed the superficial friendships Amy cultivated. She saw mourners posturing to meet Hollywood influencers who could get them their next role or replace Amy in her current film. Blonde bombshells were everywhere, many similar to Amy in looks, so it would be easy to switch one of them out for Amy.

Dressed in subdued garb, no one recognized Zelda, giving her the opportunity to overhear whispers of conjecture that Amy's aunt killed the starlet to get her money. If the police got wind of it, they could bring her in for questioning. With no money of her own and being the sole beneficiary, the motive would be clear. Amy's staff and entourage would testify that Zelda was looking for the will and living off of her niece, just another parasite hanging on to a famous person. However, the suspicion might shift to the unknown letter writer if she turned it over to authorities.

Zelda put the letter in her purse. She'd visit the police station tomorrow.

❦ 10 ❦

By Wednesday, the construction workers had finished ahead of time and cleaned the space of dust and debris. Kim came in behind them and put the finishing touches on the vendor areas while Autumn sent out an email to all the vendors letting them know they could move into their spaces starting Thursday. She hoped most of the commotion would be over before Dana Wood arrived on Sunday.

She added a phone call to her new friend, Stacey Eldridge, who owned the local bookshop. Stacey was highly creative, and Autumn couldn't wait to see what she had planned for her space, especially with a Halloween theme. Her dog, Clay, a liver-colored toy poodle with hair clipped short, enjoyed coming to the mansion and seeing Chrissy. The two fur babies looked like stuffed animals playing together. Stacey said she'd bring her inventory and decorations early on Thursday morning before she opened the shop.

As she hung up, the door opened and Steve Coleman came in with his white standard poodle, Mickey. Mickey was always well-groomed and snow white. Autumn loved his hairstyle with a big poof on his head, thick legs and body, and a pom-pom on his tail.

"Hey, there!"

"We don't get to see much of you anymore," said Steve. "You're always here. Mickey misses his morning walks with Chrissy."

Chrissy came charging across the room to greet her close friend. Mickey was Chrissy's first friend when she'd come to live with Autumn. They didn't get to play as much as usual since Autumn's work at the mansion began.

"We'll need to do something about that," said Autumn. "How about a snack, you two?"

They ran over to Autumn to get their treats. She handed them one each, which they barely chewed and swallowed.

"Was that good?"

Chrissy barked, and Mickey joined in, making a racket that echoed in the large reception area. Autumn wrote a note to get some area rugs for this space to cut down on the noise. They continued barking until they each got another treat. Water bowls waited on the other side of the desk and they headed for a long cool drink before Chrissy took Mickey into the den where she had a store of toys.

35

"Why am I the last to know?" asked Steve, leaning on the desk.

"Know what?"

"Only the biggest news to hit Knollwood since the murders and your inheritance." He smirked.

"Lisa told you?"

Lisa Coleman was Steve's daughter. She moved into his house, which was a couple doors down from Autumn's, after his heart attack.

"Of course, she told me!"

"Sorry about that. So much is going on here, I'm trying to keep everything straight."

"I'll forgive you this time. Anything I can do to help?"

"Can you take Chrissy for a walk after you have a cup of coffee with me? Walk the trails on the property and give me some feedback."

"That I can do!"

They walked into the kitchen where a fresh pot of coffee gave off a warm and welcoming fragrance to the room. They poured it into big mugs and sat at the kitchen table.

"Now this feels more like it. I miss our morning coffee time," said Steve.

"Things will get back to normal by the end of November."

"Nothing's been normal since spring, but you keep hoping."

Autumn laughed.

"Yeah, you're right about that. Maybe we can call it *Knollwood Normal.*"

They took sips of the steaming liquid. Steve reached into his back pocket and drew out a folded-up newspaper clipping. Autumn found out about the death of Chrissy's daddy from one of Steve's newspaper stories.

"Uh oh, here it comes."

"I read the paper every day. I found this buried in the entertainment section."

He handed Autumn the story with the headline,

ACTOR AMY DAVIS FOUND DEAD IN HIKING MISHAP.

"I've never heard of her," said Autumn.

"She's played minor characters in a few films and recently started getting bigger roles. The story goes on to say that she died while hiking in a hilly park with none other than Michael Williams."

"Who's that?"

"You don't get out much, do you? He's Dana Wood's husband."

"Oh," Autumn looked at the story more closely. "Poor Dana."

"Thought you'd want to know."

"I do. It makes it even more important for her to have a peaceful visit. Let's not bring this up while she's here."

"Agreed. I'm sure Lisa's cooking will put her at ease, too."

"You just reminded me we need to know if she has a special diet. I hope my contact knows."

Chrissy and Mickey came running into the back hallway near the kitchen, a look of urgency, followed by pawing at the back door.

"That's my cue. I'll take these two out."

"Thanks, Steve."

⚜

Beatrice and Elizabeth arrived at the same time and chatted as they walked up the front path to the mansion. Even in jeans and casual tops, these two looked put together.

"Hello, ladies," Autumn greeted.

Chrissy ran over to them, wagging her tail. She sniffed the air to see if there were any treats, but all she got were loving pats and sweet talk.

"I like that you're both dressed for an attic adventure," said Autumn.

"I've been looking forward to this," said Elizabeth.

"Me, too," Bea chimed in. "A trip down memory lane."

They mounted the winding stairs to the second floor where the attic door was halfway down the hall. Chrissy did her best to navigate the hardwood steps. Autumn worried she might slip one of these days, and had stair runners on order to make it easier for Chrissy to climb. In the meantime, she scooped up her little bundle, kissing her head while they ascended. Chrissy sat calmly in her mommy's arms.

Autumn pulled the attic key from her pocket. It was safer to keep the door locked when guests were here. The door creaked as it opened.

"Spooky," said Elizabeth with a smile.

Kim appeared out of one of the bedrooms.

"Can you please spray this door with lubricant when you get a chance?" asked Autumn.

"Sure thing!" she said, closing the guest room door behind her. "Beatrice, great choices on the bedding. Thanks for helping me this morning."

"This morning?" Autumn questioned.

"It was early, and I wasn't here that long," said Beatrice.

"This house is so big and the walls are so thick, it's easy to sneak around here," said Autumn.

"I did nothing of the sort!" Beatrice feigned offense.

Autumn found the light switch inside the doorway and flicked it. They climbed the wide attic stairs. Bare bulbs hung along open beams, their light barely reaching the far edges of the space. Shadows consumed the areas around the perimeter. They'd need a flashlight to explore what lay in wait in those dark piles. The smell of mothballs and old cloth filled the massive attic that ran the length of the mansion. The wood cathedral ceiling soared above them, and dirty arched windows spaced twenty feet apart let in dim light. Dust motes floated in the rays of sunlight. Clear paths on either side of the attic between piles of books, furniture, paintings, and God-only-knew what else allowed access up and down the extensive store room. It was the equivalent of a string of garages at a storage facility, maybe larger.

Autumn still held Chrissy. Until she determined if there was anything dangerous up here, like mouse traps, nails, or splinters, Chrissy would stay safe in her arms. Autumn inspected the floor, which needed sweeping, not confident that Chrissy's little paws were safe. She spotted a baby carriage tucked between dress forms and trunks, pulled it out from its nest, and tested its strength. Satisfied, she plopped Chrissy onto the white satin cushion edged with ruffles inside the carriage. The sides were low enough to allow Chrissy a view of the space and high enough to keep her safe.

Autumn heard the door below swinging back and forth. She peered down the steps and saw Kim spraying the hinges and eliminating the creaks.

"If you're curious, come on up," said Autumn.

"I love attics! Thanks!" said Kim as she bounced up the stairs.

She looked around, turning her head and body to get the entire scope of the place. Shadows at the end of the room hid whatever treasures were down there.

"Man, these windows need cleaning. And look at this floor! I'll get on it."

Kim ran downstairs for cleaning supplies and came back with what she needed, for now. Tackling this the way she wanted would take weeks of concentrated effort.

"This is like a treasure hunt!" exclaimed Elizabeth.

"We'll need to organize this stuff at some point..."

"I'll help!" said Kim from her position bent over a dustpan.

"Great! But until then, let's stay focused on anything we can use for Halloween. Let's split up."

"I brought flashlights," said Beatrice, handing one each to Autumn and Elizabeth. "Sorry, Kim, I only have these."

"No problem. I have my hands full anyway."

The women went in different directions. Autumn pushed the Chrissy carriage along the cleared walkway toward the far end of the attic toward the biggest window in the space. Cobwebs softened the window frame. Something scurried and caught Chrissy's attention. Autumn saw a beautiful view of the trails she created, seen through the treetops. She liked the patterns created by the winding paths through the woods.

"Elizabeth?" Autumn called out.

"Over here," Elizabeth answered from the far center wall.

"I want to show you something,"

Elizabeth walked through the obstacle course of objects from where she was to where Autumn stood.

"As you look out various windows up here, think about where we can put the fake tombstones." Autumn pointed out the window. "There are the trails. Wherever you think it makes the most sense is fine."

"A graveyard is a great idea! I'll check it out from up here and on the ground."

"Also, keep your eyes open for anything you find that we could use in a scavenger hunt."

"Okay. When I get closer to Beatrice, I'll tell her, too."

Autumn gave her the thumbs up and started looking in her area for Halloween treasures. Chrissy, parked next to the window, watched the goings on in her yard.

Stacks of leather-bound books with gilded letters, upholstered chairs, some with signs of wear, bird cages, and white sheets thrown over items that made them look like ghosts. Autumn turned to check out another area and came face-to-face with herself. Startled by her mirror image, she jumped, heart pounding.

"Scaredy-cat," she scolded herself.

The full-length mirror stood on a carved stand made of red oak. It was perfect for Dana Wood's suite. She dragged it out from the corner and closer to the stairs.

Behind the mirror was a large brown trunk. It made a brittle cracking sound when Autumn lifted the lid. A faded floral pattern decorated the inside of the trunk. It contained gowns of satin in deep shades of rose and violet and others of ivory and pink lace. She pulled one out and walked to the mirror, seeing herself as from a bygone era.

There were enough gowns for herself, Bea, Elizabeth, Stephanie, Kim, and Lisa to wear to the extravaganza. Hopefully, they were the right sizes.

Kim was still sweeping every spot on the floor she could manage and knocking down cobwebs with the broom. This was a project like the basement was, with the books and such. It would take months to go through this stuff and make piles for donation, sale, dumpster, and keep. Autumn was happy to have Kim to help and planned to invite Stacey up here to inventory the books. Stephanie would want a piece of the action, too.

"Bingo!" yelled Elizabeth.

Autumn wheeled Chrissy to where Elizabeth stood, and Beatrice hurried to join them. Kim put down her broom and dustpan to check it out.

Elizabeth had found the Peabody family Halloween trove of decorations. Statues, Halloween village miniatures, paper and ceramic pumpkins, witch dolls both standing and flying on broomsticks, vintage signs depicting kids having wholesome fun by bobbing for apples, owls with glowing eyes, and life-size scarecrows. Orange twinkle lights filled several large boxes. They found costumes in a trunk stored amidst the decorations. It was a mix of the past and present.

"All we need to purchase are cornstalks and tombstones! These decorations are amazing and rare. If you found them in an antique shop, they'd cost a fortune," said Elizabeth.

"I found the Christmas ornaments and decorations at that end," Beatrice pointed.

"I guess there is some organization to all of this after all," said Autumn. "As far as the costumes, we can use these traditional witch and monster outfits, or we can wear the period gowns I found. You're all welcome to choose."

"Let's get everything downstairs," Beatrice said, taking charge.

Everyone grabbed as much as they could carry. Autumn picked up Chrissy and put her downstairs on safe ground before going back upstairs and loading herself with items.

"I also found this mirror to put in Dana's room. Ray and Adam can get that down the stairs."

"That belonged to Aunt Agnes," said Beatrice. "When she started gaining weight, she banished it from her room."

The women laughed.

"I'll make sure it's spotless," Kim promised.

They loaded up the elevator and put everything in the living room. From there, Elizabeth could organize and decorate.

Finally, they brought down the trunks with the gowns and costumes and lugged them into the bedroom where Autumn planned to sleep while Dana and Gail were here. Too tired to try anything on, they decided to regroup the next day.

❦ 11 ❦

Susan DiMarco clipped the article from the tabloid and affixed it under the plastic page in her photo album. Michael Williams, with his arm around Amy Davis, irritated her. Poor Michael, being suspected of Amy's death. And Amy's name was everywhere, in print and on the tongues of Hollywood partygoers. If Michael had killed Susan while they were dating, would the fame she craved like a drug addiction have increased?

Depicting Dana Wood as an innocent victim of a cheating husband made Susan grimace. Dana was never home, always flying here and there to make a movie, leaving Michael all alone. Now there were rumors of divorce, and Susan expected Michael to turn to her. He hadn't. It wasn't fair. None of it was.

And where did that leave her? Alone, accepting minor roles that gave her face recognition but not her name. Unless Michael wanted to rekindle the magic of their intense but brief romance. They cut it off when news that Dana's latest film wrapped, and she was on her way home. When Dana left for her next project seven months ago, she'd waited, but he didn't call.

Next thing she knew, Michael was gallivanting around town with Amy for all to see. He wasn't as brazen with her as he turned out to be with Amy. They went out in public together. With Susan, he met her at her house, or they took long drives to deserted beaches for their amorous trysts.

Relationships in the film industry are everything. When Michael sought a new romance, the contacts she had through him dried up, and so did the projects he recommended her for. Susan's own blonde-and-beautiful look was common in Hollywood, so she brought nothing exciting to the screen. Not like Dana Wood. Her exotic beauty and ability to transform herself into whatever character she played was unmatched by most, especially those of Susan's caliber.

She slammed the cover of the thick photo album shut. As she was deep in rumination, the phone rang four times before she answered. It was her agent, Mel Argento.

"Hey, Mel."

"Don't sound so thrilled to hear from me."

"Rough day."

"Then this news will give you a lift."

Susan's heart pounded in her chest.

"Tell me!"

"I just got off the phone with the casting director of Albert Holton's latest film. I convinced him to give you a shot."

She squealed with excitement.

"Don't get too crazy, now. I sent him headshots and a few clips from some of your recent projects. He wants to cast you as one of the creatures in his new mystery fantasy, *Dark Hollow Road*.

"A creature!" She was horrified.

"It's a great opportunity to meet some East Coast contacts and to work with Albert Holton, and, wait for it, Dana Wood!"

She went silent. Dana Wood. She couldn't get out from under the shadow of the woman. Besides, this meant Michael was alone, again, and she could make a play for him.

"Hello?"

"Yeah, I'm here. Don't you have anything here in L.A.?"

"Nothing right now. At the very least, it's a paycheck."

If she took the part, maybe she could weasel her way into a bigger role or get Albert Holton to cast her in his next project as a supporting actor. Maybe even become the understudy for Dana Wood herself.

"Susan?"

"Yeah, I'm here."

"Whattaya say?"

"Where am I going?"

"New Hope, Pennsylvania. You'll be staying in a cute B&B in the center of town called the New Hope Inn."

"Oh, boy."

"It's beautiful there in the fall. Leaves changing. Cool air."

Susan sighed.

"When do I leave?"

⚡ 12 ⚡

Autumn saw that Chrissy stayed out of the way of the foot traffic through the grand foyer. It wasn't much better outside, with Ward Everly building the hay bale maze, so she curled up in her favorite spot on the window seat.

The only person in the living room was Elizabeth sorting the decorations and updating her drawings. When Autumn went to check on her precious little girl, her head lay on a pillow with her eyes closed and her breathing was slow and even. Elizabeth saw Autumn in the doorway.

"No worries, mom. Your baby is quiet and comfortable. I'm keeping an eye on her."

Autumn smiled.

"Thank you. She's not used to this much commotion."

Autumn cut down on some foot traffic by having those with booths closest to the emergency exit downstairs come in and out that way. The others came through the foyer. She went down to the basement to see how everyone was making out.

"Hey, Stacey! I didn't see you come in."

"The emergency exit is a lifesaver. Books weigh a ton."

Autumn scratched Clay behind his ears.

"But you have Clay to help you."

"All six pounds of him. He weighs less than some of these volumes."

"These giant spider webs and carved bookcases make it look like a magical library from a witch's house."

"My witch costume will hit that concept home. I made a special hat with veiling and glitter. Clay is coming as a bat."

"Can't wait to see that!"

Autumn waved as she walked past the other vendors selling everything from glassware to jewelry to food. Those with perishables set up the shelving and display cases, but didn't put out their wares.

Lisa Coleman waved her over.

"I'm imagining these cases filled with your desserts," said Autumn, salivating.

"This whole area is great! It looks positively medieval down here with the stone walls."

"Thanks. I'm hoping all twenty vendors feel the same way."

"I heard them talking. They're as excited as I am about the event and happy to have an indoor auxiliary space for the big fall event."

"I'm thinking that once the inn is fully open, I'll offer permanent vendor spaces down here to make it fun for the guests."

"I'm in," said Lisa. "Let's talk about Sunday."

"I know you're super busy, and I really appreciate you cooking dinner on Sunday. We can find out if they need breakfast on Monday."

"They?"

"Her publicist is accompanying her, too, so now we have two guests."

"Can we find out about their dietary preferences?"

Autumn dialed Cheryl, Holton's assistant. She picked up on the second ring.

"Hi, Autumn."

"Hi, Cheryl. By any chance, do you know what Dana and Gail like to eat? I have Knollwood's premier chef making them dinner at the inn on Sunday night."

"I'm sure they'll appreciate that after a six-hour flight. They eat everything. That's rare these days. They should be at the mansion by four o'clock."

"Good. Enough time to freshen up and relax before dinner. Any wine preferences?"

"Dana's not a big drinker, but Gail enjoys a glass of Aziano now and then."

"How about breakfast? What time does she need to be on set Monday morning?"

"Don't worry about that. We serve breakfast to the cast. They also have transportation from the airport and for the time Dana is here shooting, so it's all taken care of."

"Okay. I'm happy to make any accommodations that come up. You know where to find me."

"Thanks, Autumn. That makes my job easier. Bye!"

"Bye, Cheryl."

Autumn turned to Lisa.

"That lets you off the hook for way too early on Monday morning."

"I'll plan the dinner menu to include all the best locally grown squash and veggies."

"With your business getting more attention, I'm thinking about a permanent chef for the inn. Could you help me interview candidates?"

"Sure. I'll call The Restaurant School and let them know what the job requires and ask for student referrals."

"Someone who is good with general meals, and also makes vegetarian and vegan meals, along with desserts."

Lisa laughed. "You don't ask for too much!"

"And since we're dog-friendly, we need to serve our canine guests, too."

"Whoever gets this job has their hands full."

Autumn smiled and went back upstairs to find Chrissy waiting at the top of the steps. Her sweet fuzzy face and sparkling eyes lit up when she saw her mommy. Autumn lifted her up and hugged her close.

"What are you doing, little one?" Autumn made loving sounds while kissing Chrissy's ear.

Chrissy pushed against Autumn's mouth and made quiet grunting sounds.

"Where's Aunt Elizabeth?"

Content in Autumn's arms, they walked through the first floor looking for Elizabeth and noticing the vintage decorations complete in the reception area. There was a ceramic pumpkin on the desk. Through the front window, they spotted Elizabeth outside talking to Ward. Joining them, Autumn saw they were in deep conversation.

"Hi, guys. The lobby looks great, Elizabeth. How are the outdoor plans going?"

"We're putting the graveyard at the exit of the maze. Ward is extending the uplights from the maze into the graveyard to give it a spooky effect."

"Love it!" said Autumn. "I'll leave you to it, then."

Going back into the house, Autumn saw the cornstalks framing the door and knew she had chosen the right person for the job.

❦

Sunday morning came. The quiet was a pleasant change from the ruckus that accompanied contractors and vendors. Ward and Elizabeth were off today, but got a monumental amount of work done in a short time. Kim and Bea did a spectacular job with the guest rooms, making them fit for the most discriminating taste.

"Let's take a walk, sweetheart," Autumn said to Chrissy.

Chrissy stepped into her pink harness. It was cool outside, but not so much as for her to need a jacket. She trotted to the door and waited for Autumn to open the door.

A rush of fall breeze entered the mansion. Ray's truck pulled up as they reached the bottom step. Ace leaped out and Ray put a leash on his collar.

"Looks like we got here just in time to take a walk," Ray said, giving Autumn a smooch and stroked Chrissy.

They entered the trail marked *Enter at your own risk!* A ghost with its arms up warned of a spooky time ahead. Ray made a *bwa ha ha* sound and wiggled his fingers, making Autumn laugh.

"Elizabeth did an outstanding job, didn't she?"

"I'll say. Folks will love this."

"Hard to believe the party is next weekend."

Ace and Chrissy walked ahead of them, sniffing the sign and then pulling their pet parents forward on the path. A man-sized scarecrow peeked out from behind the trees. Autumn saw the spotlight positioned to light him at night.

"This will look really amazing in the dark. Everything has twinkle lights and spotlights to make the trail safe, but kind of creepy." Autumn pictured it in her mind, along with people enjoying the experience.

Noses to the ground, Ace and Chrissy enthusiastically sniffed and squatted.

"How was your interview?"

"The captain treated me like the promotion was mine, but I don't want to take anything for granted. There are other candidates just as worthy."

"That philosophy is why people respect you. You've put the time in, you work hard, and you care about your colleagues. No matter what, they're lucky to have you."

"I should know something by the end of the week. I'm trying not to think about it too much."

"You'll have a marvelous distraction with Dana Wood coming this afternoon. Lisa is cooking dinner and serving us at six o'clock."

"I can't wait to find out what she's like," said Ray grinning from ear to ear.

Autumn was glad to see Ray so excited.

"Me, too. You never know until you meet someone what kind of person they are."

The gargoyle statue was just around the bend, surrounded by battery-operated tea lights. Cornstalks stood on either side of the pedestal. Farther up, a witch on a broom hung from a tree, her torn black garments flowing behind her, giving the impression of flying through the woods. Another uplight pointed at her.

The pond was just ahead, and they sat on the memorial bench to let the pups play near the water. They barked at a duck swimming on the far side of the clearing, but the duck ignored them. Ray put his arm around Autumn's shoulder. They sat in the calm, listening to birds and the rustle of leaves.

"I've been thinking," said Ray.

"About what?"

"Why are we waiting until next June to get married?"

"I think it was to have time to plan the wedding."

"If you hire Elizabeth to do the decorating, we already have the venue with the mansion. Our friends can be flexible since they're all local. What if we moved it up to December?"

Autumn looked at him in awe. She had been thinking the same thing, but didn't want to push him.

"I love that idea!" She kissed him square on the mouth and then on his cheek for good measure. He hugged her close. "Do you have a date in mind?"

"Maybe the second week so it doesn't conflict with Christmas plans."

"I'm sure we can pull this off."

"That will give me time to go through my stuff and give notice on my apartment."

"You can move things to the house whenever you're ready."

"Okay, but I want to wait until we're married to move in." He squeezed her hand.

"Whatever you want."

⎄⍺

They took the fork that led them to the end of the trail. The hay bale maze stood five bales high, making it approximately six feet, sufficient to block the view of a tall person trying to find a way out of the maze. They were tied together with the strangest knots Autumn had ever seen.

"Check it out," said Ray. "These are navy knots. I ran across them in the service. Ward built this?"

"Yes."

"I guess he was in the service, or at least a sailor. I don't know much about him."

"I don't either, but he has the most surprising skill set."

"I'm curious. He appeared out of nowhere about six months ago and established himself in Knollwood pretty fast. I'll find out next time he's here."

"Don't scare him off with an interrogation. I need him here."

Ray grinned. "I'll be gentle."

"Like a tractor trailer!"

Ray laughed.

They entered the maze, the pups leading the way. The round lights lined the walls with the electrical wires hidden within the hay bales.

"You better get the fire chief over here to inspect this before you have people in here."

"Good idea."

They made a few wrong turns, so it took about ten minutes, with the help of Chrissy and Ace, to get out, where a graveyard greeted them. Skeletons climbed out of the ground, clinging to the tombstones, some partially buried.

"This is cool!" said Ray.

The furry detectives sniffed the area, but found nothing of interest. They knew what a real human skeleton smelled like.

"It really is!"

A path led away from the graveyard, back to the driveway and the main entrance. The four of them entered the mansion and heard a crash. Ray ran toward the sound while Autumn unleashed both dogs before all three of them brought up the rear. Ray stood in the kitchen doorway staring at Lisa Coleman sitting on the floor covered in flour. Autumn, Chrissy, and Ace skidded to a halt at the kitchen entry to see the floor dusted in white powder.

Trained not to go over the kitchen threshold, Chrissy and Ace barked in unison but didn't enter. Autumn rushed to her side.

"Are you okay?" Autumn said, the alarm apparent as she shushed the pups and helped Lisa up.

"Yeah," said Lisa, grunting as Autumn supported her arm and lifted her.

The dogs barked again when they saw Lisa, so she went over to calm them, sprinkling flour from her clothes along the way. Ace licked her face, and Chrissy puppy-kissed her hand.

"I'm okay, I'm okay."

Now that they knew she was all right, Ray stifled a laugh, trying to sound concerned rather than amused. "What happened?"

"Trying to do too many things at once. My arm hit a bowl filled with flour. I'm making lemon tarts and lava cake for dessert."

With only a few hours before Dana Wood arrived, they needed to get this mess cleaned up.

"That sounds wonderful. How about you go get cleaned up, and I'll tidy the kitchen?"

"Yeah, you don't want to meet Dana Wood looking like the dough boy on television," said Ray.

Lisa shook her arms of excess flour. "Very funny." She tried to scowl at him, but ended up laughing instead. A clean smock hung on the hook outside the dusted area, along with a plastic bag. Lisa grabbed them and headed to the small bathroom off the kitchen.

Autumn had the broom and dustpan. First things first.

"Ray, can you please wipe down their paws so they don't track flour through the house?"

He lifted Chrissy, gave her a little hug, and wiped her feet with a wet paper towel. She cooperated, and Ray put her down near her bowls. She waited while Ray cleaned up Ace and told him to stay in the back hall with Chrissy. Their nails tapped on the slate floor as they went off to find their next adventure. He shut the swinging door to keep them out.

Ray grabbed a small vacuum with a hose from the utility closet and sucked up as much excess flour from the counters and floors as he could. Autumn finished wiping the counters by the time Lisa emerged flour-free.

"I'll have to go home and change before Dana gets here," Lisa said.

"I keep some outfits upstairs just in case. You're welcome to pick something."

Lisa gave a grateful nod and went back to work.

"What are we having for dinner?" asked Autumn.

"Flounder stuffed with crabmeat, asparagus, and mashed butternut squash. A fresh salad with avocado and warm cranberry honey dressing. Fresh rolls. And dessert."

"Oh, man. You've outdone yourself," said Ray.

"He is your biggest fan, you know," Autumn said.

"Okay, everybody out. I have work to do."

Security met them at the bottom of the ramp as they deplaned in Philadelphia. One of them handed an envelope to Gail, who put it in her pocket. Reporters from the local newspapers and television stations assaulted Dana with shouts and flashing cameras. Gail Armstrong had alerted the press and fed them information about the new film to detract from the problems she hoped they left back in California.

Gail allowed the press to fire off questions about the film. Dana Wood graciously answered, her smile dazzling the crowd of reporters and fans that stood outside the press circle, until the tides turned to darker subjects. "When will your divorce be final?" "Do you think your husband killed Amy Davis?" "How does it feel to live with a killer?"

Gail stepped in front of Dana, waving them all away. "That will be all for today." She handed out her card. "Contact my office with anything further."

She signaled security, who dispersed the press and the paparazzi, grabbed Dana's elbow, and guided her to the luxury sedan waiting outside the door. They sat safely in the back seat, tinted windows hiding them, and a glass barrier separating them from the driver, as the driver's assistant retrieved their luggage from the carousel and secured it in the trunk.

Gail waited until they were on their way to break the news.

"Guess who got a part in *Dark Hollow Road* at the last minute?"

Dana Wood, tired from the flight and the reporters, just wanted a shower and some quiet. She didn't feel like guessing.

"Who?"

"One of your favorite people. Susan DiMarco."

Dana groaned. "How did that happen?"

"Her agent pulled some strings. He knows the casting director."

"Great. The last time we made a movie together, she created so much drama that the director banished her from the set except for when she had lines."

"I know. I'll be on the lookout for anything she tries to pull. Don't add her to your list of worries. You have enough going on."

"I'd appreciate security at my trailer door, too."

"I'll arrange it with Holton's assistant, Cheryl. Also, Susan won't be here until the end of the week to give the main cast time to rehearse."

"Good on both counts. I've been reading over the script. It's always better to read lines with other actors."

Gail pulled out her tablet. "Now for some good news. You wanted a restful place to stay." She pulled up The Peabody Mansion Bed & Breakfast website and showed Dana.

"It's beautiful! The trees, the stone."

"The quiet. It's not officially open. Cheryl arranged it for us. Just the two of us. The rest of the cast is staying in downtown New Hope."

Dana let out an audible sigh.

"They are having a Halloween event next weekend, but that should tie in nicely with your movie promotion. I plan to take full advantage of the opportunity."

Dana took the tablet from Gail's hand and flipped through the website's pages.

"These rooms are fantastic. The current owner is a descendent of the original builder."

A picture of Autumn and Chrissy came up on the About page.

"How sweet!" Dana said. Her stomach grumbled. "Should we stop and get something to eat on the way there?"

"They have dinner scheduled for six o'clock Eastern time at the inn. Cheryl said a local chef is making dinner."

"They're thoughtful. I like that."

⊂წ∞

Cornstalks and scarecrows welcomed Dana and Gail, building their excitement as they drove down the tree-lined street and arrived at the front door of the mansion. The driver and his assistant jumped from the vehicle, helped the women out of the backseat, and pulled their luggage from the trunk. The arched doorway surrounded by cornstalks and pumpkins got Dana in a festive mood. Living in California, she had forgotten the cozy feeling of fall in Bucks County. She took a deep breath of cool air and opened the door.

A beautiful long-haired Shih Tzu greeted her at the door wearing orange satin ribbons with pearls at the center.

"Well hello there, little one." She bent down to pet her.

"That's Chrissy. I'm Autumn. Welcome to The Peabody Mansion!"

Dana extended her hand. "I'm Dana, and this is my publicist, Gail."

"It's a real pleasure to meet both of you. We've been looking forward to your visit," Autumn said, shaking their hands in warm welcome.

The men carried in the baggage.

"Thank you, gentlemen," said Dana. Gail reached in her purse for a tip.

"In front of the desk is fine," Autumn instructed. "Please, come in, and we'll get you registered."

"The place is lovely!" said Dana. "Thank you for allowing us to come even though you're not officially open."

"We're honored to have you as our first guest. Everyone worked together to make your stay as comfortable as possible."

Ray came out from the kitchen wiping his hand on a dish towel, accompanied by Ace.

"This is my fiancé, Ray, and his retired police dog, Ace. Ray's a detective in the Knollwood police department."

"Hi, Ray. Hi, Ace," said Dana. "I feel safer already."

Ray wiped his palms again before shaking hands. Dana petted Ace's head. She was used to sweaty palms when fans met her for the first time.

"Welcome to Knollwood and The Peabody Mansion." Ray said, star-struck.

"Let's get these ladies settled so they can relax before dinner."

Autumn helped Ray put the luggage in the elevator. With all the bags, only Ray fit inside the space, so he rode up and unloaded it, before sending it back down.

"I prefer to walk up this magnificent staircase," said Dana. "It's good exercise."

"I'm with her," said Gail.

Autumn and Chrissy walked up with them and showed them to their rooms. She unlocked Dana's room first and handed her the key. A fluffy king-size bed covered in a soft gold duvet gave a glow to the room. Chrissy walked right in.

"Chrissy, come here, sweetheart. Dana doesn't want you in there."

"Says who? This adorable baby can come in my room anytime."

Chrissy looked up at her. Dana swore the tiny lips smiled at her.

Ray sorted the bags and put them in her room.

"You're right next door, Gail."

The door opened onto a bright, comfortable room with large windows overlooking the woods. A sage green quilt and five coord-inating pillows decorated the queen-sized bed.

"Makes me want to stay forever," said Gail.

"Dinner is at six o'clock. We'll start with drinks and hors d'oeuvres in the living room, just past the reception desk. Dial zero if you need anything." Chrissy stayed in Dana's room. "Looks like you have a new fan."

"Go ahead, Chrissy. I'll see you later."

Chrissy looked up at Dana and reluctantly followed Autumn downstairs.

“”

Lisa laid out stuffed mushroom caps, warm brie cheese with almonds and crusty baguette, and large green seedless grapes on the coffee table in the living room. Dana and Gail appeared in the doorway. Chrissy and Ace ran over to them, tails wagging.

"Best welcome I ever had!" laughed Dana, petting each of them.

"Hi, I'm Lisa Coleman, your chef for the evening."

"I'm Dana and this is Gail. We really appreciate the meal. After traveling, I prefer a quiet evening."

Gail spotted the hors d'oeuvres.

"This is lovely!

"Just something to nosh on until dinner is ready."

"It smells wonderful," said Dana.

"Can I interest you in a glass of Aziano?"

Gail raised her hand, mouth full of mushroom cap.

Dana gave it a minute's thought. "I'll have one too, thanks."

Gail looked at her, eyebrows raised, swallowing the mushroom cap as she put another on her plate.

"You rarely drink wine."

"This place makes me feel relaxed. I don't need to have my guard up here or with these people."

"I have the same feeling," said Gail. "It's different from California. They don't seem to want anything from you except to enjoy yourself."

"Right. And these two are just too funny. They don't even beg for food."

Chrissy and Ace entertained them by playing ball in front of the coffee table.

"They already ate," said Autumn entering from the dining room holding two glasses of wine. "Aren't those delicious? I may have Lisa make them for the cocktail hour at our wedding."

"Amazing. The walnuts in the stuffing really make it special," said Gail.

"When's the wedding?" asked Dana.

"We decided to have a December wedding two weeks before Christmas. The mansion is the perfect place to have it. These two..." she pointed to the pups, "are the ring bearers."

Gail spoke up, "Please join us, Autumn."

"Thank you, I'll be right back."

She came back with a glass of wine and sat in the chair across from them. Chrissy came running over. Autumn lifted her into the roomy chair. She snuggled next to Autumn, head on her leg, and Autumn's arm around her little body.

"What a love bug. I had a Pomeranian named Paulie as a child. He was the cutest thing and my best friend," said Dana. She sipped her wine. "This is delicious."

"This is my favorite," said Gail.

"Dogs are special beings. Pure, loving, and trustworthy," Autumn said, gently stroking Chrissy.

"I think like you do, Autumn," said Dana, nodding her head. "It's much easier to trust dogs than people."

"It must be hard to trust people in your world."

Gail jumped in. "Finding the ones who want the best for you is the hardest. There's so much jealousy in our industry. Everybody wants to see you fail, except the people who make money off of you."

"I hope being here gives you a little different perspective on people. Yes, we're big fans of your work, but we measure our relationship success on how happy we make others. That includes our furry friends. The Halloween Extravaganza happening here next weekend benefits the Knollwood animal shelter."

"I saw the flyers on the desk. It sounds like such fun. I'm happy to make a presentation to encourage people to donate more than the ticket price," said Dana.

Autumn's eyes widened. "That would be wonderful, thank you!"

"Then it's settled."

"Dinner is served!" said Lisa from the doorway.

Chrissy and Ace brought up the rear as they moved into the dining room. The table was set with a gold cloth laid with crystal and gold-rimmed cranberry red chargers that were part of the Peabody china collection.

Ray held chairs out for the women and then took his own seat next to Autumn while Gail and Dana sat across from them. Autumn poured water into gold goblets and placed wine on the table. Lisa served the already-plated food and set them in the center of the chargers.

"I never expected this. It's the finest welcome dinner I've ever had," said Dana, putting the cloth napkin in her lap.

Autumn, Lisa, and Ray smiled at the compliment.

"Enjoy!" said Lisa and went back into the kitchen.

Conversation halted as the food took over everyone's attention.

"This is the best stuffed flounder I've ever had," said Gail, washing it down with wine.

"Lisa owns Coleman's Cafe on Main Street. She's a town favorite for breakfast and lunch," said Ray.

"She'll also have a vendor booth downstairs for the Extravaganza," said Autumn.

"We must check that out," said Dana.

"Are you okay with being around the public? It's only one day, but once people know you're here, we may have star gazers," said Autumn, dabbing her mouth.

"I'll have security stationed outside and inside the mansion while you're here. I can arrange for someone to accompany you wherever you'd like to go," assured Ray.

"She'll be fine on set. They have their own security. Our driver and his assistant are also part of the security team, but we appreciate the added safety you provide while Dana is here," said Gail.

"Adam is one of my best officers and is dating Autumn's best friend, Stephanie. The two of them could provide casual cover and show you around town."

"I'll keep you apprised of Dana's schedule. Until she starts filming, we won't know her schedule."

"But I'll try to be here for the Extravaganza," said Dana, taking a bite of the mashed butternut squash.

"We'll only need coffee in the morning," said Dana, thinking she'd have a full stomach for days after this meal. "We leave at dawn."

"Lisa's fresh croissants and some fruit will be available, just in case," said Autumn. "Ray and I are staying here, so if you'd like something more substantial, we can take care of that, too."

Chrissy made her way over to Dana and stared at her.

Dana offered her some fish, but she turned her nose up and walked away.

"She's just curious about what you're eating. She doesn't like fish or vegetables," watching Dana's shocked expression.

"How long does it take to shoot a film?" asked Ray, between bites of fish and crabmeat.

"This one will likely take about three-and-a-half months to film in totality," said Gail.

"Then you'll be here for the wedding," said Ray, scooping salad onto his plate.

"Great! You're both invited, along with anyone you'd like to bring. Lisa is catering the reception, and it's taking place here," said Autumn.

"Any chance to eat whatever Lisa's making works for me," said Gail, following suit with the salad.

"I'm in! In the meantime, Gail and I will rarely be here. We work between twelve to sixteen hours a day, five days a week," Dana clarified. "They feed us and provide transportation. I'll just need to get in whenever I get back."

"We'll give you a spare key tonight. If you need anything, we're staying in the rooms at the end of the hall."

Lisa came in to clear the dinner dishes and prepare for dessert.

"Coffee or tea with your dessert?"

"Herbal tea for me," said Dana.

"Coffee, please," said Gail.

Lisa looked at Autumn and Ray. "I know what you two want."

Autumn followed Lisa into the kitchen.

She brought back a tray of coffee, a selection of herbal teas, cream, sugar, and honey. She placed China cups and saucers in front of each person. Lisa came out with a tray of lemon tarts and chocolate lava cakes.

"That looks like what's going to put me over the top," said Gail, patting her stomach.

"I want both, so how about we share?" asked Dana.

"Works for me. Lisa, you've outdone yourself," Gail said sincerely. "I'll recommend your services to the catering coordinator on set."

Lisa's eyes widened.

"I'd love that! Sure." She dug in her apron pocket and handed Gail a business card. "Thank you."

"Will you be cooking for us on weekends?" asked Dana.

Autumn looked at Lisa, waiting for an answer.

"Absolutely," Lisa blushed and practically hopped back to the kitchen.

"There are lots of things to do in the area when you're off," said Autumn. "I'll put together some information and leave it in your room."

"Sounds good," said Dana, licking her lips.

It was getting late, and the inn's guests politely covered their mouths and yawned. Autumn picked Chrissy up and brought her over to say goodnight. Autumn gave them keys to the front door of the mansion. Ace accompanied them to their rooms. Ray and Autumn went into the kitchen to help Lisa.

"They were really impressed," said Autumn.

"Maybe Dana will take me back to California with her and make me her personal chef."

"She better not!" Autumn said, lightly pushing Lisa's arm.

"Wow, Dana Wood is coming to our wedding! Aren't you glad we moved it to December?" said Ray.

"You what?"

"Oops, I guess the caterer needs to know about these things," Autumn put her hand to her mouth realizing her error.

"Uh, yeah!"

"It's two months away. Look what you expertly pulled off with less than a week's notice," Autumn reminded Lisa of her amazing talent.

"True," Lisa blew on her nails and rubbed them on her shirt giving herself kudos.

"I'll set the coffeemaker for five in the morning," Lisa promised.

Ray called to Ace. "I'm going to make a last patrol around the property before we head to bed." He kissed Autumn and then Chrissy, and squeezed Lisa's arm. "Great job tonight!"

Lisa's smile was so broad both her top and bottom teeth showed.

⚡ 14 ⚡

Autumn was up by four AM to ensure her guests had what they needed. She and Chrissy saw lights under everyone's doors, including Ray's. Autumn picked up her little girl to give her a sense of security as they descended the stairs. The stair runner should arrive any day now, and then Chrissy could go down the steps on her own.

The smell of fresh-brewed coffee wafted from the kitchen. She let Chrissy out the kitchen door to relieve herself, keeping a careful watch to ensure no animals approached her. She chose a spot at the edge of the woods and came running back in.

"You're such a good girl!"

Chrissy padded over to her water bowl and took a long drink.

Autumn made little trays for Dana and Gail with mugs of coffee, packets of sugar, and a little crystal creamer. She put a warm croissant on each tray with a knife, pats of butter, and a little bowl of homemade blueberry jam from the farmer's market.

"Let's bring these upstairs, sweetheart."

Autumn grabbed the trays and used the elevator this time. Chrissy sat calmly inside the cab as though she'd been riding elevators all of her life. They arrived at Gail's door first. Chrissy gave one sharp bark, and Autumn put one tray down and knocked.

Gail answered fully dressed. The computer was lit up on the bed.

"Good morning," said Autumn. "Where would you like this?"

"Good morning. You must have read my mind. On the table next to the chair, please."

Chrissy followed her mommy into the room and looked up at Gail.

"Good morning to you, too, Chrissy."

She wagged her tail.

"There's more downstairs."

"Thank you."

The pair walked down to Dana's door. Autumn knocked. Chrissy barked. Dana, also fully dressed, seemed a bit tired this morning. Even without makeup and jet lagged, the woman was exquisite. Autumn sensed that her glow came from the inside. She felt Dana's warmth in every interaction.

"Good morning," Autumn said brightly.

Dana took the mug from the tray.

"Now it is. Jet lag is the worst thing about traveling." She took a sip of coffee. "Mmm. Perfect."

Chrissy barked and waited for Dana's response.

"Hello, sweetheart. You're such a beautiful little girl." Dana put her mug down and picked up Chrissy, giving her a gentle hug. Chrissy's tongue lolled in enjoyment.

Autumn put the croissant tray on the coffee table in front of the sofa.

"How did you sleep?"

"Wonderfully. I just wish I could have stayed in bed longer."

"I didn't realize how demanding the movie industry is. Hopefully, you'll get back tonight at a reasonable time so you can get some sleep."

"Tonight we'll probably get back here around nine o'clock. We're reading through the script and going through the shooting schedule." She kissed Chrissy's ear, put her down, and picked up the coffee mug. Chrissy shook to put her hair back into place.

"We'll let you get ready. C'mon Chrissy."

Chrissy looked at Dana.

"I'll see you later, sweetheart."

Chrissy wagged her tail and followed Autumn down the hall. She knocked on Ray's door. He opened it, and Ace greeted them first. Ray bent around Ace to give Autumn a kiss.

"Coffee's ready. Can I bring you some?"

"I'll come down. Ace needs to go out, and I want to do a perimeter check before the limo arrives."

Autumn petted Ace and picked up Chrissy. Ray and Ace followed them down the winding staircase.

"We'll be right back for that coffee," Ray said, opening the front door.

A package the size of a shoe box sat on the front step. It was gift wrapped with a fancy purple bow. There was no card as far as Ray could see. He put his arm out to stop Ace from sniffing it.

"Let's go out the back door, buddy," he said while pulling out his cell phone.

He led Ace through the kitchen and out the back door. Ace picked the spot where Chrissy went earlier and covered her scent with his.

"Come on back in, Ace." Ray patted his leg to get the dog's attention. The dispatcher picked up at the other end of his call. He recognized the voice.

"Hey, Norma. It's Ray."

"Good morning," she said.

"I'm at the Peabody Mansion. We have a VIP guest staying here. I found a mysterious box on the front step this morning. It may be nothing, but I don't want to take a chance. Can you please send someone from Ordnance Disposal over here?"

"Sure thing. Getting in touch with the officer on call."

"Thanks, Norma. Have a good day."

"Stay safe." She clicked off.

Autumn was getting his coffee.

"Don't let our guests go out the front door."

His furrowed brow worried Autumn. She rarely saw him like this. She handed him a mug. He took a sip.

"What's wrong?"

"There's a package out front. Someone put it there after we went to bed. I called the bomb squad, just in case. Don't let anyone, including Chrissy, out the front door."

He put the mug on the granite countertop.

"I'll check the back and sides of the building and wait for the limo."

Autumn grabbed the coffeepot and trotted up the stairs with Chrissy close behind. She knocked on Gail's door first. Gail opened the door chewing the croissant, a smidge of blueberry preserves at the corner of her mouth.

"More coffee?"

"Yes, please."

"What time is the limo arriving?"

Gail looked at her watch.

"In about fifteen minutes. Why?"

"Ray was checking the outside and found a suspicious box on the front step. It could be nothing, but he'd like you to stay inside while he waits for the limo and gives the okay to come out through the back door."

"Oh, my!"

"He's got everything well in hand, but let's err on the side of caution."

"Yes! I'll tell Dana."

"We'll be in the kitchen, if you want to come wait with us."

Gail nodded, washing down the croissant with coffee.

"Also, please call when you leave the set to come back. Ray will ensure everything is okay at this end."

"Will do." Gail put down her mug on the dresser and jogged down the hall to Dana's room.

Autumn heard the urgent discussion between the women as she went back downstairs.

By the time Dana and Gail came down, two police cars were in the driveway, red and blue lights reflecting off the building. The bomb squad had the gift box safely contained. With the area secured, they pulled away.

Ray and Ace patrolled the outside one more time before the limo arrived. From the front living room window, Dana, Gail, Autumn, and Chrissy watched him talk to their security detail assigned to her limo. Autumn let Dana hold Chrissy for comfort.

"I'm wide awake now!" said Dana, a touch of humor in her voice.

"Too much excitement, too early," said Gail.

"Ray will get to the bottom of it," assured Autumn.

"I wonder if Susan is already in town," said Dana.

"Who's Susan?"

"Susan DiMarco. An actor who has an extreme dislike of Dana. It's jealousy."

"Enough to harm her?"

"You never know."

"I'll give her name to Ray to check it out."

The limo was ready. Dana and Gail grabbed their bags. Ray and Ace escorted them to the limo and tucked them into the backseat. He nodded to the bodyguard in the front seat as they drove off.

Autumn stood in the doorway holding Chrissy.

"I'll let you know as soon as the bomb squad finds out what's in the box. What do you have on the schedule today?"

"Vendors are still working downstairs, and I'm going over the final decorations and events with Elizabeth. Kim is coming to clean the guest rooms."

"Let the vendors use the emergency exit downstairs and keep the main floor basement door locked."

Ray kissed Autumn goodbye and loaded Ace into his Knollwood Police SUV.

Exhausted from getting up so early and the morning's excitement, Autumn cradled Chrissy and went back upstairs for a nap.

C3&0

Elizabeth and Autumn sat on the couch in the den. Chrissy snuggled between Autumn's leg and the back cushion. She snored, waking herself up periodically and once again drifting off to sleep.

"I've never put together a scavenger hunt," said Autumn hoping for guidance.

"We make a list of things for participants to find. They'll be things already set up around the event to ensure that participants get to see everything. For example, we could put 'gargoyle' or 'flying witch' on the list, so they'd have to walk down the trail to find it."

"I like it."

"Each person gets a souvenir trick-or-treat bag they can reuse on Halloween to collect the proof that they found the item. We can put baskets at the base of each item filled with squares with a picture of the item or just the word of the item."

"There will be kids here, so let's make it appropriate for them and fun for the adults."

"Then a picture is best so the younger children can associate the picture with the target object. I can find clip art online and put it on a cardboard backing."

"The first five individuals or teams who make it back with a full checklist get to choose a carved pumpkin to take home."

"We'll certainly have enough of them after Stephanie's fifth graders go to town on their project."

"If you want to splurge, we could order pens branded with The Peabody Mansion B&B and a phone number or web address."

"The event is this Saturday. Isn't it too late for that?"

"I have a local friend in the business who will take care of it. And her stuff is excellent quality."

"Order a thousand of those in different colors. Please tell your friend she can put her business cards on the promotion table in the lobby."

Elizabeth made a note.

"I'll walk through the property and create the scavenger hunt list and ask Ward to hide something in the maze. I'll also set-up a candy table in the reception area using the Halloween bowls and skulls we found in the attic."

"Don't forget the doggy treats. Crunchy and chewy."

Elizabeth wrote it down.

"Where shall I set-up the step-and-repeat banner?"

"What's that?"

"You see them on the red carpet shows behind celebrities with the logos of the sponsors of the event. I ordered one with The Peabody Mansion B&B in your signature font. It's about eight feet by eight feet.

We'll put a red carpet in front of it. You can use it permanently and create a guest photo wall behind the desk."

"Let's put it in a corner of the living room so it doesn't block traffic in the reception area. Do you know a professional photographer to go with the backdrop?" Autumn was getting excited about the event.

"Sure do."

"One more thing. I know it's probably your busy season, and short notice, but can I book you for the second week in December?"

"That is my busiest time with Christmas decorations."

"You could even do it earlier, in November, right after Thanksgiving, if that's easier. Ray and I moved up the wedding date. We don't want to wait until June."

"How exciting! Congratulations! Where is the venue?"

"Right here. I'd like a winter theme that we can leave up through the holidays."

"That can be arranged. Thanks for choosing me."

"We make an excellent team, I trust you, and I like your aesthetic. No need to look further. Whatever the occasion or holiday, you're the one I want to work with, so please put me on your permanent schedule."

Elizabeth laughed.

"Happily! We also talked about leaving the cornstalks and pumpkins through Thanksgiving and removing the spookier stuff. Is that still the plan?"

"Yep. And you can have the run of the attic to put away the old and search for new. Beatrice found the Christmas decorations up there, so you have a head start."

Chrissy moaned and stretched. Autumn scratched her side, and she rolled over on her back, exposing her tummy to get the most out of her mommy's attention.

C380

Kim was disappointed that Dana had left before she arrived for work. The woman fascinated her. Even her younger sister, Hannah, was a huge fan. She wanted to get an autographed picture for her.

Kim propped open the door to Dana's room and wheeled in the cart. The bed was slept in but the duvet barely rumpled. Dana must have slept soundly with little movement. Kim fluffed all the pillows, even the unused ones that were piled neatly on one side of the bed. She left a piece of wrapped dark chocolate truffle when she finished making the bed.

Dana's empty suitcase stood on the floor of the full closet. The dresser drawers were full. Autumn mentioned that Dana would be here for months. She must be accustomed to traveling and making herself at home wherever she stayed.

After dusting the entire room, Kim swept the hardwood floor that surrounded the luxurious area rug, which she vacuumed. She went into the attached bathroom. Dana's lotions, creams, makeup, and other sundries sat organized on the counter. The welcome basket, shampoo, conditioner, and handmade lavender soap from a local lavender farm, were on the shelf in the damp shower. The purple mesh loofah hung from the hook on the shower shelf. The used white bath towel hung on the door hook to dry. It was going to be easy to keep up with Dana during her visit. Kim gave the entire bathroom a thorough cleaning.

Back in the bedroom, she found Chrissy sitting on the rug, looking around. This morning she wore orange, black, and white satin ribbons with rhinestone centers.

"Are you waiting for me?" Kim cooed.

Chrissy wagged her tail. Kim removed her rubber gloves and stroked Chrissy's soft head, wishing her own hair was as nice as Chrissy's. Maybe she should try the organic honeysuckle shampoo Autumn used on her precious puppy.

"Let's go, sweetheart. We have another room to clean."

They walked down the hall to Gail's room and used the master key to open the door. It looked like a *clutter-bomb* had exploded. That was the term Kim's mother used when she wanted Kim to clean her messy room, and it stuck with her. Clothes were strewn on the chair and the bed and pouring halfway out of the suitcase. Makeup stood around on the dressing table and on top of the dresser. The bedding looked like ten people had rolled around in the bed. A piece of exercise equipment sat on the area rug. Shoes lined up near the closet, but not in it.

"Wow, Chrissy. We have lots of work to do in here."

Chrissy sniffed the clothes and the shoes, jumping back and sneezing after exploring one particular pair of flats.

"Ripe, eh, little one?"

Undeterred, Chrissy sniffed the edge of the bed and the threshold of the bathroom, but didn't go in.

"That's not a good sign. Will I need a hazmat suit?"

Kim started in the bathroom. She replaced the damp towel she found on the floor with a fresh one. She lifted and pushed the counter clutter so she could wipe everything down.

When she came out of the bathroom, Chrissy had gone.

She wasn't sure if it was housekeeper protocol for strewn clothing, so fought the urge to hang up the clothes. Instead, she cleaned around the clutter. To make the bed, she moved the clothes draped across it and put them on the chair. She turned to find a piece of paper on the floor. It must have fallen from the pocket of a jacket she moved. She picked it up and read the note scrawled across it.

We're going through with it. Saturday night. Be ready.

It was unsigned.

An icy chill ran through Kim. The note had a sinister undertone and the scratchy handwriting looked evil. Maybe she was making more of it than necessary. Saturday was the Halloween Extravaganza, and Autumn wanted everything perfect. She would tell Autumn and Ray. Or should she? Had she broken the privacy of a guest and likely get in trouble, possibly losing her job, which she desperately needed and also loved? She couldn't be sure of what it meant, or which Saturday it referred to, so should probably stay out of it.

Years ago, she overheard one side of a phone conversation her father was having, misinterpreted it, and ruined her mother's surprise birthday party. She swore that, or anything like it, would never happen again.

Yes, stay out of it.

She tucked the note into the pocket of one of the jackets laying on the chair, finished making the bed, and got out of there, locking the door behind her.

Ray and Ace were walking down Main Street when he got word that the package found on the front steps was a teddy bear holding a heart and a love note to Dana written in a heavy hand, the letters pressed deep into the notecard. There was no signature.

You have my heart. You have my soul. You have my watchful eye to keep you safe.

Maybe it was from a fan who truly cared about Dana. It could also be from a stalker. They often targeted celebrities. Lots of people knew Dana Wood was in town, but how many of them knew where she was staying? And why deliver the box in the middle of the night? Only someone who wished to stay anonymous until he or she revealed themselves would do that.

Ray texted Dana's security detail to give them an update. They assured him that Dana was safe and in a protected room going over the script.

Cautious being Ray's middle name, he couldn't be sure that the people on the set were trustworthy. Whoever wrote the note might be sincerely looking out for Dana. Or maybe they wanted her for themselves. Stalkers lived in their own bubble, with their own rationale to go with it.

He called Adam and alerted him to the situation, then scheduled two officers to take the overnight shift outside the mansion.

Across the street, Ray saw Ward Everly enter the hardware store. Ray and Ace crossed and entered Hector's Hardware behind Ward. Hector saw them and greeted them with a handshake for Ray and a cookie for Ace, who gobbled it down and turned a hopeful eye to Hector for another one. Ray kept this eye on Ward.

"Good boy, Ace. I have more for you back here," said Hector.

"That's nice of you, Hector. Could you watch him for a minute?"

"Always here for my buddy, Ace. Come on."

Ace followed him behind the checkout counter where Hector kept the box of dog cookies.

Ray followed Ward into the plumbing isle. Ace came around the corner of the same aisle at the opposite end blocking Ward's exit.

"Hey guys. What's going on?"

"Hi, Ward. How's it going?"

"Picking up some supplies to fix Maureen Roberts' kitchen sink."

"You really get around."

"Try to. Seems I'm the only handyman in town. Lucky for me I landed in the right town."

"How long have you lived here now?"

Ward put his finger to his chin.

"Been here for quite some time."

"You did a nice job on the maze, especially that knot work."

"Learned that in the Navy. Comes in handy."

"I'm a Marine. Served in Afghanistan before being discharged."

"My last duty station was San Diego. Easy compared to what you went through."

"I'll say."

"Gotta get back to Maureen's house. See you around, Ray. Ace."

"Take care. Come on Ace." Ray watched to see if Ward signed a credit card authorization, but pulled out cash instead, so he called out from the door, "Bye, Hector! Ace says thanks for the cookies."

"There'll always be a box waiting for him." Hector waved as he rang up Ward's purchase.

Ray loaded Ace into the SUV and sat for a few minutes thinking about Ward. He'd lived in Southern California, one hundred twenty miles from Los Angeles. Ray wondered if Dana ever had ever seen him before. Ward was one of many fans who could have sent the stuffed bear. Maybe there was a way to get a handwriting sample to match up with the love note.

He dialed Autumn.

"Hello." She sounded groggy.

"Did I wake you?"

"Yeah. Chrissy and I went back to bed after everyone left. She is lying here, looking at me."

"The box from this morning wasn't an explosive."

"Thank goodness! What was it?"

"A stuffed bear with an unsigned note for Dana. I'll bring it back once forensics goes over it."

"Everyone coming on Saturday will sign the guest book. We can check the note against the book."

"Good idea. I talked to Ward. He used to be in the Navy and lived in Southern California. He wasn't clear on how long he's been in town. I don't have any cause to suspect him, but let's keep an eye on him."

"Will do."

"I ordered two officers to watch the outside of the mansion overnight. Ace and I will be over by dinnertime."

"Okay. I should probably get up. Lots to do before Saturday."

ೞ

Autumn took a few moments in bed with Chrissy, rubbing her head and kissing her ears. Chrissy grunted and stretched, putting her paw on Autumn's arm, the love between them palpable. One more little squeeze, and Autumn pushed herself out of bed, jumped in the shower, dressed, brushed Chrissy, and adorned Chrissy's pigtails with black satin bows with little skulls in the middle.

"You're so beautiful!" Autumn squealed and kissed the top of her head.

Chrissy beat her tail against the floor. Autumn scooped her up, and they went downstairs. Elizabeth came out of the den holding a pile of paper with colorful images.

"Good morning!" said Elizabeth.

"Hi. What do you have there?"

"The scavenger hunt list. Check it out." She handed one to Autumn and reached out to pet Chrissy.

The orange and black frame had ghosts, witches, and vampires floating around the list that had both pictures and text. The picture of a gargoyle also said *gargoyle* next to it. Each item had its own box and a place to check-off the found items. From her pocket, Elizabeth pulled a few of the squares she made as proof of the found item.

Autumn perused the list.

"This is wonderful!"

Elizabeth smiled and placed the pile on the side table near the reception desk.

"I'll give these out on Saturday evening."

"They should be fine there for now. I'd like you to announce that the hunt is on."

"Along with instructions how it works. Can't wait! And Stephanie called to say the pumpkins are being delivered tomorrow. That gives me time to light them up and place them in the best spots."

"I bought another big bag of battery-operated tea lights, just in case you need more. They're in the back hall.

"I'm taking this little munchkin for a walk. Want to join me? We can walk the trail and check everything out."

"Can't say no to that."

≈ 16 ≈

Dana and Gail arrived back at the mansion around nine o'clock. The building was a beacon lit from the eves to the ground. Two uniformed police officers stood at either end of the building to ensure Dana's safety.

"I thought you said it was just a stuffed bear," said Dana.

"Detective Reed isn't taking any chances," said Gail.

The security detail helped them from the limo. Ray opened the front door, Ace at attention beside him.

"Good evening, detective," said Dana.

"Please call me Ray."

"I appreciate the effort, but is all of this really necessary?"

"Yes," said Ray, leaving no room for argument.

Dana shrugged.

Chrissy charged at Dana, wagging her tail at the actor.

"What a friendly welcome!"

Dana bent down and petted the Shih Tzu. Chrissy ran from the room and came back with her ball.

"Dana's tired sweetheart. She'll play with you later," said Autumn. Then to Dana, "How was your first day?"

"It went well. There was good energy between the actors. Albert is a genius with getting everyone working together."

"I hope he has the same effect on Susan when she gets here on Wednesday," said Gail, putting down her computer bag.

"Hungry?"

"I could go for a little something," said Dana.

"Lisa made her soon-to-be-famous chicken pot pies. Get settled, and I'll bring it up to your rooms."

"I haven't had one of those in years," said Gail, grabbing her bag and heading up the stairs.

"Sounds perfect," said Dana, and trudged up the steps.

Chrissy went to follow her.

"Stay with Mommy, sweetheart."

Chrissy gave her a pouting look.

"Want a treat?"

Chrissy's short attention span forgot about Dana and focused on treat. Ace looked hopeful.

"You, too, Ace."

They followed Autumn from the reception area. She got them settled with some jerky treats in the back hall and made trays for the ladies that included a giant chocolate chip cookie and hot herbal tea. Ray helped, and they took the elevator up. Chrissy and Ace stood at the top of the stairs.

"This isn't for you," said Ray, knocking on Gail's door.

Chrissy followed Autumn to Dana's room. When the door opened, Chrissy slid inside.

"My biggest fan," laughed Dana. "I don't mind having her in here."

Autumn put the tray on the coffee table.

"I'm glad since I haven't had any luck stopping her."

"She's sweet."

"When do you start filming?"

"More rehearsals first. We'll know better once the rest of the cast arrives. Albert showed me the stretch of road we're using as Dark Hollow Road. It's beautiful with the leaves changing colors."

"You came at the perfect time of year."

"It won't look like it does in person in the film. Nothing in the movies is quite what it seems with all those special effects."

"Will it be another early morning for you?"

"We'll leave around six o'clock."

"Coffee and croissant, then?"

"Yes, thank you."

"Okay. Sleep well. Come on, Chrissy. Aunt Dana has to eat and get some rest."

Dana petted her goodnight, and she followed her mommy out the door.

Ray and Ace waited at the bottom of the steps.

"That room looks like a cyclone went through!" he whispered.

"Dana's room is super neat. Gives us a preview of the variety of guests we'll have when we're fully open."

"We're going to patrol the outside." He kissed Autumn, who held out Chrissy for a goodnight kiss. He smooched her ear.

"We're going to bed. Please don't stay up too late. You still have a regular job to do."

⊰⊱

Zelda Weems didn't like being questioned. She insisted that Amy was more use to her alive, despite being her only beneficiary. And what about the letter she handed over? Didn't that count for anything?

There could be someone out there waiting to kill again, and here she sat across from two detectives throwing questions at her.

Since the initial investigation, the detectives determined that Amy's head injuries were from a blunt object, not just hitting rocks as she fell off the cliff. She was likely dead by the time she hit the ground. They considered Zelda and Michael their best suspects so far. The two closest people to Amy who had the most to gain. Zelda with the money and Michael protecting his money and marriage to Dana Wood.

Zelda argued that the letter showed that someone other than her had a reason to harm Amy. They didn't like what she was doing with Michael. But lots of people knew about the relationship. It could have been anybody, and celebrities had no shortage of threats.

The detectives wanted to know where Zelda was the day Amy died. Did she give Amy a black rose? She told them she didn't know. She was in a haze from her insomnia medication and couldn't remember. Zelda listed the side effects of the drug: memory loss, confusion, disorientation. They reminded her that aggression was also one of the severe side effects of the drug.

Zelda had no alibi. No one could vouch for her whereabouts around the time Amy fell to her death. Admittedly, she came out of her mental fog to find herself following Amy down the street on more than one occasion. Amy would tell her to stop taking her meds, that Zelda was an embarrassment, but Zelda was hooked. In those moments, she hated Amy.

She couldn't remember seeing Michael or Amy on the day of Amy's death. Yet it was plausible that she could have followed them to the hiking trails in a stupor. She didn't want to give the detectives any ammunition, since they didn't have enough to keep her in custody. They released her after three stressful hours. Perspiring and anxious, she headed home to take a shower and pop an anxiety pill along with her insomnia medication.

❧ 17 ❧

Susan DiMarco arrived for rehearsal on Wednesday, and the calm shifted into angst. Susan demanded jelly beans and sparkling water be available and complained that she didn't have a private trailer like Dana.

She snapped at the script supervisor, argued with the wardrobe assistant, and turned up her nose at Dana. Puzzled by her attitude, the East Coast crew avoided her. They especially disliked her treatment of Dana, who they had gotten to know as friendly, cooperative, and fun to have around.

The friendship the casting director had with Susan's agent, Mel Argento, was now in severe jeopardy. Horrified at the woman's behavior, he texted Mel to let him know that his client was causing trouble, and not to ask for any more favors. As he typed, Susan found a new target to unload on. Within minutes, Susan's phone rang.

"What's your problem?" asked Mel, controlling his outrage.

"I don't have a trailer, my costume is trash, and these people are unprofessional!" Susan yelled into the phone.

"Listen, Albert Holton has a spotless reputation, unlike you. I had to pull strings to get you this gig, so just shut up and cooperate."

He heard her growl into the phone.

"Let me put it this way. If you don't cooperate, consider our contract void."

"You wouldn't."

"Your contract is at my discretion. I have the right to release you if I determine you're not the right fit for my agency."

Silence at the other end of the phone.

"Tell them you're jet lagged and need a day of rest before starting fresh in the morning."

Nothing.

"Susan?

"Fine."

She hung up.

Mel texted the casting director and asked if Susan could start the next day. It was fine with him. Anything to get this woman off the set. He told Susan to come back tomorrow, and she stomped away, jumped into her compact rental car, and drove back to her hotel.

"Okay, everyone. Deep breaths. Shake it off. Let's skip to where Dana's character finds her brother."

Some mumbling ensued as they flipped pages to the right scene. Dana's voice hit the perfect tone for the scene, and everyone relaxed.

⊂3∞⊃

Susan stormed into the lobby of the New Hope Inn, yelled at the clerk to bring her more towels, pounded up the staircase to her inadequate room, and slammed the door. She knew the star, Dana Wood, was likely staying at a high-end hotel. And they stuck her here in a small room with a queen-sized bed, thin quilt, and tiny bathroom. It was all beneath her.

Why did Dana Wood have everything Susan was supposed to have? Her entire life as she envisioned it belonged to the A-list actor. Not one person recognized Susan DiMarco in this small, stupid town. People should turn their heads to get a glimpse of her. The local press should have met her at the airport. Where were the paparazzi to follow her around and get her story?

Susan's film roles were minor, but she gave it her all, waiting for acknowledgment. Even in the movie databases, they listed her halfway down or near the bottom of the cast and crew section. Playing secondary characters gave her some audience recognition, but only the sense of remembering that she briefly played so-and-so on a television show. They didn't know her name, but saw the milky skin, blonde hair, and blue eyes so common in her profession. They always cast her as that type.

Why didn't the director ever see that she could transform herself into something other than a bimbo with a wig or makeup effects? She got her wish in this film. The creature costume and makeup they showed her in the mock-up set her off. Covered up like that, no one would know who she was. Transformed into the creature, her hopes of making it big in an Albert Holton film fell to the ground, just like Amy had.

Dating Michael should have put her over the top. He was no longer interested in her. He didn't return her calls. She'd tried many times after Dana left on Sunday, but he didn't pick up. He didn't return her messages. Her anger rose. By the time she flew out of LAX, in coach sitting next to a mother and a crying baby, she'd reached a crescendo that carried into her tantrum this morning. At least people noticed her as she yelled at the baby to stop crying. The flight attendant moved her to an aisle seat in coach next to an elderly man. The baby stopped crying.

Sulking in an upholstered club chair, Susan had a realization. Demanding what she wanted didn't work. Trying an alternative approach might be best for her career. With Mel Argento mad at her and threatening release from her contract, she needed to be careful. He was the last agent who'd taken a chance on her. The others booted her, too.

Tomorrow, she'd watch Dana and see how she won people over. Susan would put on the best performance of her life as the cooperative, happy, gracious person people wanted to see. A whole new start awaited her.

Ϗ΀

Susan returned to the set Thursday morning, ready to work. The actors and crew cringed when she stepped out of her rental car. Her smile took them off-guard. Her apologies for her behavior yesterday surprised them. They assured her they understood how exhaustion affects people and gave her latitude.

The production secretary cautiously gave her the day's schedule and showed her where she could get breakfast.

Susan searched the room for Dana and saw she was having breakfast with Albert Holton. They were engrossed in conversation. She observed Dana's open body language, smile, and easy laughter. Crew members looked at ease interacting with the person in charge of the production, and the one with the most influence, approaching their table with questions, exchanging smiles, and enjoying the interaction.

She smiled at everyone as she moved down the buffet, filling her plate. She even acknowledged the server, something she never did. People gathered around tables, reviewing the work for the day. She scanned the room to see where she belonged. Susan's first impulse was to sit with Dana and Albert, but there was an unspoken boundary over sitting with them unless invited.

A table of minor actors sat laughing and enjoying their breakfast. She sighed. For now, that's where she belonged. As she approached, they looked at her expectantly. She guessed that they waited for an outburst, so she kept smiling.

"Is this seat taken?" she asked politely.

She saw their eyebrows raise and lips pressed together.

"Nope, it's all yours," one of the male creatures said.

"Thanks."

The creatures quietly watched Susan take her food from the tray and set it on the table.

"Where is everyone from?" she said, taking a forkful of scrambled eggs.

"We're all local," said a female creature. "How about you?"

"I'm from L.A. The jet lag is brutal. Sorry about the fuss I made yesterday. That's what happens when I'm overtired."

They nodded and ate their pancakes and eggs. Some drank their orange juice. She felt they used the food and drink to avoid commenting on her behavior.

She continued to try dialogue with them. "Is this your first time working with Albert Holton?"

"We're his first string of actors he calls when filming a new project. He's a great guy. It's a privilege working with him," said another creature between chews.

Susan nodded. "Good to know."

No one mentioned working with Dana Wood, and she decided not to ask. Maybe they felt contempt for her the way she did.

"What is there to do around here on the weekends?" asked Susan.

"This Saturday is the Halloween Extravaganza at The Peabody Mansion. We're all going. The word is, Dana Wood is staying there," said the female creature.

Susan controlled her facial expression. She smiled instead of grimacing.

"That sounds like fun. I'd like to go."

"Ask the production manager for a ticket. It's a charity event for the local animal shelter, so they bought a bunch of tickets to support the cause."

"Thanks for the tip."

Susan's mind reeled at the possibilities the event brought her.

⚡ 18 ⚡

Chrissy snored under the desk, and Kim's cart rumbled on the landing above. Autumn knew Kim had a lot of work upstairs with two official guests plus Autumn and Ray, especially the one guest that required the work of several guests.

Autumn flipped her auburn hair behind her as she went over the final to-do list. The extravaganza was two days away, and there were lots of last-minute details to tend to. She took great joy in checking off completed tasks and lowered her stress by adding to the list so she wouldn't forget anything. Elizabeth's organizational skills put her much further along in the plans than she could hope for doing it alone.

The front door opened, and Mickey poked his long, white nose through the door, followed by Steve Coleman. Chrissy jumped to attention and skidded around the desk to greet her friend. Their tails wagged furiously. Autumn had the image of their tails flying off from the pace. Chrissy took a moment to say hello to her Uncle Steve, who rubbed her vigorously on the chest.

"Hello there!" said Autumn, pleasantly surprised.

"You're never home anymore. We miss you. I grabbed your mail."

Steve put it on the counter.

"I'm glad you made the trip. How about some coffee and one of your daughter's croissants?"

"Sure."

"And snacks for these two. Let's sit in the living room."

Chrissy and Mickey were already playing in her toy pile, searching for the perfect item to play tug of war. Mickey's strength was no deterrent for Chrissy, and Mickey let the princess think she was winning.

Steve settled himself on the couch and enjoyed the woodland view through the Palladian window. Autumn brought in a tray.

"Did you hear about the scare we had?"

"It was on the front page of the Knollwood Gazette. Must have scared the daylights out of you."

"Ray had everything under control and kept Dana safe. No one got hurt, that's the important thing."

"Just goes to show you never know what might happen from one minute to the next."

"I read that Dana is giving a speech at the extravaganza to support the animal shelter."

"That was in the paper? Gail was the only one there when Dana made the offer. She must have sent a press release."

"It showed Dana Wood in a good light. Now that folks know she'll be here, there will likely be twice the number of people you're expecting."

"Then Ray needs to double the security, too."

☙❧

After morning rehearsal, Dana went to her trailer and checked her messages in voicemail, text, and email. She hadn't expected a text from Michael, begging her forgiveness and threatening to end his own life if she didn't stay with him. She wrote back that she wished him well, but it was time to move on, and recommended he call his therapist to guide him through their divorce. Then she texted her manager, Ken Blanchard, and asked him to check on Michael when he got a chance.

Meanwhile, Gail arranged to maximize Dana's role in the Halloween charity event and worked with the wardrobe department to get a white, tattered and fitted ghost gown with veiling for Dana's costume. Everything was right on schedule and according to plan. It would be the publicity shocker of the year.

Hours later, Dana and Gail got back to the inn around nine o'clock with the same level of security as the night before, a yummy, light dinner, and kisses from Chrissy. Dana felt right at home here and couldn't think of a better place to spend the next three months.

After settling in, she reviewed her messages and heard the voicemail from Ken Blanchard asking her to call him. It was only six thirty in the evening in California, so she dialed his number.

"Hi, Ken."

"Dana. How are things going?"

"The inn is great and everyone here is friendly. All except Susan DiMarco."

"What's she doing there?"

"Mel Argento knows the casting director."

"Great."

"I'll deal with it. Your message sounded like you had something important to tell me."

"Are you sitting down?'

"Yes."

"Dana, I'm so sorry to give you this news."

"Ken, you're scaring me. What's up?"

"It's Michael. After you asked me to check on him, I went over to your place. He didn't answer the door, so I used the key."

"And...?" She had stopped breathing.

"I'm so sorry."

"Stop saying that!"

"He was in his study, lying on the floor. The gun next to him."

"Is he at the hospital?"

"The coroner took the body."

A sob caught in Dana's throat.

"When?"

"They weren't exactly sure. I told the police about the text he sent you. That puts the time of death as this morning."

"He only threatened to kill himself. Oh, God! I told him it was over between us and that he needed to get help. It's all my fault!"

"No, no. It's really not. Don't blame yourself. He left a note."

"What did it say?"

"That he killed Amy Davis and his life was a mess. He took the blame for losing you, and he couldn't go on without you."

Dana sobbed into the phone.

"What can I do, Dana?"

"I need to notify his mother."

"The police already did that."

"I'll call her."

"Okay."

"Should I come home for the funeral?"

"You'll get mobbed by reporters. The story hasn't broken yet. Do you want me to let Gail know?"

"I'll tell her. Thanks, Ken." Dana sniffed into a tissue, tears streaming down her face.

She hung up and covered her face with her hands. As soon as she caught her breath, she walked down the hall to Gail's room and knocked softly. Gail's face dropped when she opened the door and pulled Dana inside.

"What wrong?" Gail said as she made room on the chair for Dana to sit.

"It's Michael."

"What's he done now?"

Dana could hardly get the words out.

"What?" Gail squatted in front of her, touching her leg.

"He..." Dana's lips quivered, "killed himself."

Gail fell back on her heels.

"Dear, Lord." She whispered. "I never thought he'd go that far."

"He sent me a note threatening to do it unless we got back together."

"This is not your fault!"

"That's what Ken said. It's also what Michael's suicide note said."

Gail squeezed Dana's arm.

"You can't go back to California right now."

"I'll call his mother and see if she needs help to arrange the funeral."

"And I'll do damage control. I hope no one besides the police saw that note."

"Ken did."

"I'll call him and tell him to keep his mouth shut. He likes to spread bad news."

Gail picked up the house phone and called Autumn.

"Hi, Gail," said Autumn, chipper despite the hour.

"Do you have any more of that chamomile and lavender tea? Dana could use some."

"How about you?"

"Any of that wine left?"

"Coming right up."

Autumn and Chrissy took the elevator up and brought the tray to the guest rooms. They knocked on Gail's door first and delivered the wine. Chrissy led the way to Dana's room. She opened the door, her face drawn and tear-stained. Chrissy marched into her room. Autumn put the tea and a biscuit on the table.

"Are you okay?"

"I got terrible news." She hesitated. She didn't know Autumn that well and didn't want the news to spread too soon.

"I'm a good listener when you want to talk about it."

Chrissy pawed at Dana's leg, and Dana picked her up and snuggled her.

"And so is Chrissy."

Dana held onto Chrissy, putting her face in the soft hair. Chrissy licked her face.

Autumn went into the bathroom and put cool water on a washcloth.

"Here, this will make you feel a little better."

Dana handed Chrissy to Autumn and wiped her face. It did feel better to clean the tears away. Autumn handed her a tissue, the trashcan, and then gave Chrissy back. Dana hugged the sweet Shih

Tzu. Dana let out a deep sigh. Autumn knew the calming power of holding Chrissy.

"Take a sip of tea before it gets cold."

Dana did as she was told.

Autumn dimmed the lights.

"Thank you," said Dana softly. "And thank you, sweetheart." She kissed Chrissy's ear and gave her back to Autumn.

"Rest well," said Autumn, gently closing the door.

⚹ **19** ⚹

Susan DiMarco heard that Albert Holton had told Dana to take the next couple of days off. They could work on other parts of the production to give her a chance to mourn. Maybe the director would notice her without Dana Wood around. Dana Wood. Everyone kept saying poor Dana. She was divorcing Michael anyway. She didn't care about him.

Everyone seemed so concerned about Dana. No one cared about Susan and her needs.

Michael Williams' name was all over the entertainment websites. No one had cared about him until he died. Was death the secret to fame? If she died tomorrow, would they plaster her name all over the web in bold headlines? There was no mention of her in the articles about Michael. Amy Davis. Dana Wood. Nothing about Susan DiMarco. As a secret lover, no one witnessed her involvement with Michael, so didn't include her in the stories.

The heck with them. She'd make sure her name got out there.

ⳗ

Dana stayed in bed longer than she had in years. The bed was so soft and the sunlight perfectly filtered through the flowing curtains.

The heart wrenching late-night call with Michael's mother left her feeling wrung out. The woman didn't want a public spectacle made of her son's death, so she decided on a private farewell. Dana offered to pay for it, but Michael's mother refused. She thought Dana had already done more for Michael than he deserved.

It surprised Dana that her mother-in-law didn't blame Dana for Michael's demise. She realistically blamed Michael. He had it all and threw it away. She assured Dana that his self-destructive tendencies were already there when Dana met him, and not because of anything Dana did. It astonished her that the marriage lasted as long as it had.

Mrs. Williams ended the call with praise for Dana, her pride in Dana's accomplishments, and her sadness at how shabbily Michael treated her. Dana wished her well and promised to stay in touch.

A gentle knock on the door disrupted Dana's thoughts.

"Are you awake?" Gail asked softly.

Dana reluctantly threw back the covers, put on her thick terry robe, and answered the door.

"Did I wake you?"

"No, just lying in bed thinking."

"Don't think yourself into a depression. There was nothing you could have done."

"I know. Even his mother doesn't blame me. It's sad to think of a life wasted, but otherwise, I'm fine."

"Good, because Michael's death is all over the Internet, but no one is blaming you."

"What are they saying?"

"That it's because he killed Amy Davis and couldn't live with himself. Most of the tabloids say it's a good thing you left to film a new movie before he killed you, too."

"I don't believe he killed Amy, and he never threatened me."

"But the press doesn't know that. We need to direct the narrative away from you and toward his infidelity."

"Please don't make his reputation any worse on my account."

"He did that on his own."

"I'm hungry," said Dana.

"Get cleaned up, and we'll head downstairs. Autumn is making eggs over easy in a bagel and bacon."

"Perfect for a fall day."

⊂≋⊃

Gail left the room to find Kim in the hallway.

"Hello, I'm Kim, the housekeeper."

"I'm Gail. You're doing a great job."

"Thank you. Let me know if you'd like me to do anything extra for you, like put away your clothes."

Gail smiled.

"My room is a bit messy, isn't it?"

It was Kim's turn to smile.

"Sure. Have at it. We're going downstairs for breakfast, so the rooms are available."

Kim nodded.

Dana came out of her room. Kim froze.

"Dana, this is Kim, our housekeeper."

Dana extended her hand.

"Nice to meet you, you're doing a wonderful job."

Kim slowly raised her hand to meet Dana's.

83

"Uh, wow, uh, I was hoping to meet you. I love your movies, and we're so glad you're here, and if there's anything I can do for you, uh..." Kim stammered.

Dana patted her on the shoulder.

"I appreciate that, especially since I'll be here for the next few months. We'll see a lot of each other."

"Thank you, uh, that's great, oh, wow!"

Dana gave Kim her famous, glowing smile.

"My sister is a huge fan, too. She'll be here on Saturday."

"I'd love to meet her. See you later."

Gail admired Dana's skill at making people feel tended to while making an exit.

They descended the grand staircase and crossed the foyer. The smell of bacon and eggs drew them to the dining room where orange juice and coffee awaited them. Chrissy appeared next to Dana wagging her tail.

"Hello, little one."

Gail shook her head.

"You're getting attached."

"This little girl makes me feel lighter and happier. I can't explain it."

Autumn came in with two plates loaded with food.

"She did that for me, too. When I got her, my parents and I were in a car accident that resulted in their deaths, and she calmed me down and helped me manage the PTSD and the grief of losing them. As a survivor of the crash, the flashbacks came on suddenly. Chrissy somehow knew it was coming before it hit full force and barked until she brought me back from the vision. She's amazing."

"I knew there was something special about her," said Dana.

"You have no idea."

Autumn waited a moment then said, "I'm sorry for your loss."

"Thank you. And for yours, too."

"If you'd like to take a walk after breakfast, the trails are lovely and the trees have a soothing effect."

"Are the officers still outside?" asked Gail.

"You bet. Including Adam Miller. He'll accompany you on your walk."

Dana nodded.

"Let Aunt Dana eat. This isn't good for babies."

"She can have some."

"Thanks, but she doesn't eat table food. It upsets her tummy. Enjoy!"

Autumn picked up Chrissy and left.

◌৪৩◌

Autumn opened the front door and called for Adam. He hustled over to her.

"You guys need coffee or anything?"

"No, thanks."

"You're finally going to meet Dana."

"Oh, man. This is amazing."

"She and Gail might take a walk in the trails after breakfast. Would you mind keeping an eye on them?"

"Of course. So far, it's all quiet out here. Ward is putting some finishing touches on the maze, and there's an officer out front in his car."

"Stephanie will be over later with the pumpkins. Elizabeth is meeting her here to place them. Kim will be here all day, and vendors will probably come in and out of the emergency exit downstairs setting up for tomorrow."

"It's going to be mobbed for the event. Everyone's talking about Dana being here."

"The cast and crew of *Dark Hollow Road* are also coming. Albert Holton bought everyone tickets."

"You'll set the animal shelter up for the next twelve months after this shindig."

"Hope so."

"I'll wait for them outside."

Autumn went back inside and cleared the dishes as the women sat patting their stomachs.

"Hit the spot," said Gail.

"I do want to take that walk," said Dana. "Mind if I bring Chrissy along?"

Chrissy's tail slammed into the floor.

"Take advantage of having the place to yourself before tomorrow. I'll get her ready."

Autumn put Chrissy's pink fleece sweater on her, then held out the soft harness. Chrissy stepped into it and waited while Autumn attached the matching rhinestone leash. Dana watched in amazement.

"This is the most well-behaved dog I've ever met."

"She is quite something," agreed Gail.

Autumn kissed Chrissy's head.

"Enjoy your walk, sweetheart."

85

Autumn handed the leash to Dana.

"She likes to chase squirrels and chipmunks, so please keep her on the leash."

Dana nodded.

"Adam is waiting outside the front door."

Autumn watched Adam's eyes grow large when he saw Dana.

"Miss Wood! It's so nice to meet you."

Dana put out her hand, and Adam took it gently in his and covered it with his other hand.

"The pleasure is mine. This is my publicist, Gail."

Adam tipped his hat.

"You're in for a real treat down the trails."

He looked down.

"You'll show them the way, won't you, Chrissy?"

Chrissy wagged her tail.

"Ladies first."

Chrissy trotted ahead of the group, hips swaying. They walked past the entrance to the hay bale maze and saw Ward Everly testing the lights. He looked up.

"Miss Wood. Such a vision I did not expect on this lovely morning. I'm Ward Everly, jack of all trades and maze overseer."

"Nice meeting you."

He looked at Gail.

"I'm Gail."

"I see you already have protection, so I'll sit this one out. Adam's a good man."

Dana waved as they entered the trailhead. She chuckled at the *enter if you dare* and *ghost crossing* signs. The trees gave them a show, raining their colorful leaves upon the trail.

Gail said, "This is going to look spooky with the twinkle lights lit.

"It's beautiful back here. And I get to enjoy this for the next few months. I've missed the change of seasons."

"When did you live on the East Coast?" asked Gail.

"When I was in my late teens. I lived about an hour north of here in Easton."

"And I thought I knew everything about you."

"Not everything." Dana winked at Gail.

Chrissy stopped ahead of them, sniffing the ground, then looked up when she heard rustling in the leaves. She listened intently for a moment. Satisfied it was nothing she wanted, Chrissy once again scampered down the path.

They came upon the bench and the pond. The dedication to Autumn's parents touched Dana's heart and made her think of Michael. He was lost at the end. Their industry was soul-sucking. It happened to many whose dreams were dashed. Michael was incapable of managing his money and relied on Dana way too much. She was ready to end the heaviness he brought to her life, but he found a way to hang onto her heart. She wondered if she could continue living in the house where he took his last breath.

"Penny for your thoughts," said Gail.

"Of all the places I've been, Pennsylvania makes me feel comfortable, lighter. Maybe it's the trees. Or the people."

"It is a different feel here. Even on set with local actors and director. Well, until Susan DiMarco brought her energy into the mix."

"I could live anywhere, don't you think? It doesn't have to be in Los Angeles."

"You're rarely there anyway."

"If you're thinking of checking out properties around here," Adam said, "you can consult Autumn's favorite realtor, Maureen Roberts."

Dana considered this information. When Adam said it, something clicked in her, and her body relaxed.

"I'll get her number from Autumn."

"You're seriously going to move here? What about the snow?"

"It's cold, yes, but so beautiful."

"The town and surrounding areas make sure the roads are plowed. If you get stuck and need to get out, just let one of us know. Plenty of folks around here have trucks and SUVs."

"Or I could buy one myself."

The pieces fell into place. Gail looked at her.

"Don't worry. We can still work together. We've done it when I'm overseas. Why not from Pennsylvania?"

Gail's mouth opened, and then closed.

"It is nice here. And you seem happier somehow."

"Maybe Albert will put me in more of his films if I'm local. He only shoots in Pennsylvania."

"That's true." Gail gave her a dazzling smile.

They came to a fork with signs pointing to the hay bale maze or to the loop that continued the woodland trail.

"I'm up for the maze," said Gail.

Dana made a left and found the path leading to the maze.

"How many entrances does the maze have?" asked Gail.

"The fire chief insisted that there be an entrance in the front, one from the trail, and one from the cemetery. We also have to keep an eye on the number of people in there. And no smoking anywhere on the grounds or in the house," said Adam.

"Safety and no smoking works for me," said Dana.

Chrissy led the way, sometimes hitting a dead end, but eventually coming out the exit at the graveyard. A woman straightened some tombstones and tilted others.

"Hi, Elizabeth," said Adam.

Her eyes got big when she saw Dana.

"This is Dana Wood and Gail Armstrong. Ladies, this is our holiday decorator extraordinaire, Elizabeth Johnson."

"Wow, this is such an honor," Elizabeth said, unable to contain her excitement.

Dana flashed her famous smile.

"Did you create this?"

"I did. It's been such fun working on this project."

"This is as good, if not better, than some of the professional set decorating I've seen," said Dana.

"Really? Thank you! That means a lot coming from you."

"If you're up for it, I can float your name by the local production managers. Do you have a card?"

Elizabeth's hand shook as she reached into her pocket and handed Dana her business card.

"I really appreciate this."

"I can't promise anything, but Gail will take some photos so we can show them your work."

Elizabeth's hands went up to her mouth. Dana loved giving deserving people an opportunity to succeed beyond their wildest dreams. It made her as happy as she made them.

Chrissy pushed on Elizabeth's leg.

"I didn't mean to ignore you, little one." She caressed Chrissy's head and scratched behind her long ears.

"Should we go back through the maze to get to the front?" asked Gail, snapping a few photos.

"You can take this path through the cemetery and back out to the driveway."

"Take care," said Dana with a wave.

Elizabeth waved back.

Ward Everly stood at the end of the graveyard path, wiping his hands on a rag.

"Did you enjoy yourselves?"

"It's incredible," said Gail.

"Wait until you see everything lit up at night."

Chrissy pulled on her leash, wanting to go back to the house.

"You miss your mommy?" asked Dana.

They waved at Ward as they headed back. Adam noticed Ward giving hard looks to Dana. He delivered everyone to the front door and stayed at his post outside.

"There's my baby!" Autumn exclaimed as though she hadn't seen Chrissy for days.

Chrissy ran over to her. Autumn unhooked the leash, removed the harness, and undid the Velcro straps on Chrissy's fleece. She shook her long hair. It fell into place.

"I wish my hair could do that," said Gail, laughing.

≈ **20** ≈

Saturday morning, only hours before the public arrived, everyone ran around putting last touches inside and out. Kim raked the red, orange, and brown leaves from the trail. Food vendors put products in their booths, Ward switched on the outdoor lights, and Elizabeth took one last walk through the spaces to ensure perfection.

Candy adorned a large round table in the entry foyer, strategically placed pumpkins started on the front steps, into the foyer, and down into the basement, the scavenger hunt set-up, and the photo backdrop installed. The scheduled speakers would deliver their presentations from the spider-webbed podium in the living room. Rows of folding chairs lined the room, and Knollwood Animal Shelter posters stood on easels on either side of the speaker area.

A red velvet rope hung across the stairway and also blocked the elevator, alerting guests that these areas were off limits.

Dana and Gail were upstairs, resting before getting into their costumes.

Stephanie walked through all the spaces to ensure it was safe for kids. Her colleagues let her know that the Kindergarten through second grade children planned to come at the start of the event with their parents. Her own class wanted to see their carved pumpkins lit up at night, so they'd come later. Stephanie saw their excitement at knowing the event would give their work as prizes. Since they planned to enter the scavenger hunt and win, they could pick their own pumpkin or one they liked better.

An officer stationed at the Peabody Museum directed cars into the parking lot there. A museum staff member wearing a milk-maid costume complete with white bonnet welcomed them with programs for the Halloween Extravaganza and a discount coupon for the museum.

Beatrice came for breakfast with Dana and Gail. She charmed them and told Dana about her exceptional experience selling her house with Maureen Roberts. Autumn saw her joy when the ladies commented on the beautiful bedding in their rooms. Now Bea was changing into one of the antique gowns in Autumn's room. She was in charge of the money box and ticket sales until volunteers from the animal shelter showed up.

Jasper volunteered to keep her company at the ticket table, dressed in period garb he found at a shop in New Hope to match the era of Bea's gown. It emphasized Jasper's gentlemanly good looks, like he was born to that time in history.

Those who were at the mansion now were there for the duration, except for the police officers who guarded the place on the main floor, in the basement, and outside. Their shift would change around seven that evening.

Chrissy was comfortably curled in her fluffy bed under the desk, with Mickey dozing next to her, to escape the noise. Autumn needed to keep an eye on her when the partyers arrived.

Ray and Ace patrolled outside. On a leash, Ace looked even more authoritative and majestic, silently warning people to stay in line. As such, Ray chose not to put him in costume. Instead, Ace wore his old police uniform from before his retirement.

Steve Coleman was downstairs helping Lisa set-up. He also volunteered to help Stephanie monitor the scavenger hunt prizes.

Vintage gowns awaited Stephanie, Elizabeth, and Kim upstairs. Autumn lifted Chrissy from her bed and hugged her close, cradling her head as she unhooked and replaced the velvet rope on the stairs. She knocked on the door, warning Bea she was coming in. Bea stood in front of the mirror admiring herself. Autumn put Chrissy on the bed.

"You look beautiful!"

"I feel incredible in this."

"It's like it was made for you."

The cranberry silk with ivory lace gown fit Bea's curves perfectly and made her skin glow.

Autumn helped sweep up her hair in a loose bun and helped her with some makeup. She loved seeing Bea so happy.

"Wait until Jasper sees you," said Autumn.

"Jasper? He's just a friend who helps me with the house and gardens."

"I think he'd like a different kind of relationship."

Bea waved her away, but the blush on her cheek told Autumn she had similar thoughts.

Bea glided down the steps, the gown swishing. Jasper looked up, and his mouth fell open. He strutted to the bottom of the steps, unhooked the velvet rope, and extended his hand to help her.

"My dear, you are absolutely stunning," he said.

Bea beamed her best smile and curtsied.

"Thank you, kind sir."

Jasper offered her his arm. Autumn watched as the pair moved across the foyer with the ease of a couple who had been together a lifetime.

Autumn looked under the desk and saw Chrissy there with Mickey. She petted them both and told them to stay. She went to the basement to check on activities down there.

Autumn spotted the spooky witch's library booth draped with glittering spider webs and a giant spider navigating them.

"Stacey, you look wicked in that witch costume! And your little furry bat here is adorable!" said Autumn.

"Clay tolerates the costume, but isn't thrilled with it." She stroked the toy poodle's head.

Clay looked at Autumn with pleading eyes to get this costume off of him.

"Does he have a spot he can go to for quiet?"

"Sure does." Stacey pointed to the corner where a doggy haunted house welcomed Clay with a petite entrance, a cushioned bed, and ghosts flying around the outside.

"Your creativity is astonishing. You guys have a great day. Call my cell if you need a break, and I'll send someone down."

Steve and Lisa Coleman were deciding where they should display the crystal cake plate filled with lemon squares.

"I can settle this. How about putting it at the registration desk so they're right there when I want one?" said Autumn.

"Funny," Lisa laughed.

"Steve, Mickey is keeping Chrissy company under the desk upstairs. Can you help me keep an eye on her? I'm worried that I'll get distracted, and she'll wander off and get lost in the shuffle."

"Sure thing," said Steve. "I'll put Mickey's costume on him in an hour. He's not too fond of it."

"What kind of costume is it?"

"Superman. It has a cape. That's the part he doesn't like."

"I bought Chrissy glitter butterfly wings. When she walks, they move up and down. That works for about twenty minutes, and then she wants them off."

"Those poor babies. They'll be glad when this is over," said Lisa.

"No doubt," Autumn said with a chuckle.

"On another topic, I hired a student from The Restaurant School to watch the booth down here while I set up the refreshment table in the dining room," said Lisa. "She's an excellent candidate for your full-time chef position when you officially open the inn. Her name is Sarah Kelly."

"Thanks for the recommendation. I have to change into my costume, and so do you." Autumn pointed at Lisa. "Do you have a costume, Steve?"

He pulled out a set of red horns from his pocket and set them in place with an elastic chin strap. The horns looked like they actually grew out of his head, setting Lisa and Autumn on a tear-inducing laughing spree.

Kim, Stephanie, and Elizabeth were coming down the stairs in their gowns when Autumn reached the foyer. At the bottom of the staircase, they twirled for Autumn.

"You all look amazing!"

They flashed big smiles at Autumn.

"My turn," said Autumn, mounting the staircase.

When she got to her room the lavender and lace silk gown waited on a wall hook next to another one in an opaque garment bag. She unzipped it to find an ivory silk wedding gown with short flounce sleeves and bugle beads that formed a burst pattern starting at the center and casting out to the edges of the gown. The beading continued on the train, making it sparkle.

"Beautiful, isn't it?" said Bea from the doorway.

Autumn was so entranced that she hadn't noticed Bea.

"The most beautiful dress I've ever seen."

"I found it in the attic. It looks like the perfect wedding gown for a winter wedding."

"I'll say."

"I think you should wear it. It looks like your size."

"I love it. You're very thoughtful."

Bea beamed.

"Let's get you into the lavender dress for now. Those Victorian loop buttons are impossible to hook by yourself."

⊰⊱

When Ray and Ace came inside, Ray spotted Autumn standing at the reception table. His heart lifted, and he rushed toward her.

"You're breathtaking!" he said.

Autumn smiled and curtsied.

"These dresses transformed us. Everyone wearing them seems elevated."

Ray kissed her, careful not to smear her carefully applied lipstick.

"How is everything outside?"

"People are arriving. My officer at the museum entrance said traffic is steady. He counted fifty cars so far with two to four people in them."

"Great!"

When Ray went to get Ace, he was snoozing under the desk with Chrissy and Mickey.

Autumn noticed her circle of friends arriving. Maureen Roberts handed out business cards to advertise her realtor service as she walked through the front door and put a pile of them on the table next to those of Lisa Coleman and Elizabeth Johnson.

Brad and Julie Hall came in, holding Teddy, their Yorkshire terrier. All three were dressed as bears. They said they couldn't find anyone to dress as Goldilocks.

Stephanie Douglas came over and hugged everyone as they commented on the beauty of her dress.

Autumn was distracted for a moment, and when she looked up, she saw them going down to the basement.

୧୫୨୦

The gathering was well on its way. Droves of folks arrived, excited to see the mansion and take part in the Halloween fun. Parents with children, teens, and couples all chattered about the decorations and the beauty and size of the mansion.

Ward stood outside wearing a pirate hat, an eye patch, and a hook for his hand. A striped shirt and black pants completed the outfit. From his position, he could hear their conversations and focused his attention on what interested him. The oohs and aahs over the hay bale maze were like a pat on his back for a job well done. The bats, ghosts, and witches he'd affixed to the outside gave the structure more oomph and made people want to enter for a spooky experience.

The property got crowded quickly. A steady parade of people and pets, all wearing costumes, amused him. The hot dog costume on one Dachshund made him laugh, along with the Golden Retriever dressed as a lion. The mane matched his fur, so just for today, he got to be king of the jungle, not just king of the house.

Over the heads of partygoers, Ward looked for Dana Wood. He would wait for her to be alone before making his move.

That's what happened to Amy Davis. She was alone for a moment, thinking she was safe with Michael Armstrong, proving you can never be too careful. Amy hadn't heeded the warning he gave in the letter he sent from La Jolla.

And Dana never got the stuffed bear and his note, so she did not know his intentions.

Ward spotted her on the front steps talking to Ray and petting Ace. Her tattered gown and veil made her look mysterious and scary. The thing missing from her dress was blood. Ward took his time and waited for the right moment.

☙❧

Dana's haunting look was perfect for the event. Initially, she could go undercover with the veil, but word got around that the tattered ghost was really Dana Wood. Once discovered, Gail, dressed as a sunflower, was ready with the photos, a Sharpie, and a sign-up sheet for Dana's mailing list. Elizabeth had a table set up in the reception area for Dana to sign autographs. They only had forty-five minutes before the presentations about the animal shelter, but in that time, the pile of photographs had gone to her many fans.

People gathered in the living room, filling every chair and squeezing against the walls. Autumn was up first, thanking everyone for coming, going over the schedule of events, and reminding people to visit the vendors downstairs.

Autumn introduced the director of the shelter, Carly Jones, who was the first presenter. She showed photos of happy pups and cats waiting for adoption. She told of the rigors of running a shelter and the funding needed to provide food and medical care to the animals. She told interested pet parents to stop by her table in the back of the room to fill out an application and make an appointment to come meet their future best friends or to make a donation.

Autumn went back to the podium and emphasized that while the proceeds from this event benefitted the shelter, they greatly appreciated donations. Then she introduced Dana.

"In the short time she's been here, Dana Wood has shown us her love of animals. Chrissy and her friends have gotten many pats and treats since Dana arrived."

As though cued, Chrissy, wearing her butterfly wings, came charging in toward her mommy, stopping at Dana's feet, tail wagging. Dana lifted her up to show the crowd.

"Case in point," said Dana, and kissed Chrissy's ear.

"No need to say anything else. I yield the floor to the incomparable Dana Wood!" finished Autumn.

The room burst into applause.

Dana handed Chrissy to Autumn, who noticed glitter on her head.

"Thank you, everyone. I feel so welcome here. Not only in this town, but at The Peabody Mansion Bed and Breakfast. Autumn's hospitality is unmatched and enhanced by Chrissy's affection. They make me feel at home. Chrissy has lots of friends who come and visit, showing me how special each of them are. Each breed has special qualities, whether purebred or mixed, and each one has its own personality.

"The reason these beautiful dogs express themselves so sweetly is because they have stable homes and loving pet parents. You could be the one who makes a difference to a lonely animal looking for someone to love.

"I encourage you to open your wallets, but also your hearts and homes, and become part of the pet parent community, if you're able to devote time and attention to a fur baby.

"My travel schedule doesn't permit me to be a responsible pet parent, so I'm fortunate to have Chrissy to visit with. She was a resident of this same shelter before Autumn adopted her. Chrissy was lucky to only spend one night in a cage. I think of those sweet furry souls sitting at the shelter and want them to find joy. In the meantime," Dana summoned Carly Jones to the stage with a wave of her hand, "here is a check for ten thousand dollars to get whatever the shelter pets need to be happy while they await their forever homes."

Carly's jaw dropped. She hugged Dana.

"Thank you so much, and thanks to all of you for your generosity. Have a great time!"

"I'll be taking photos with donors over at the red-carpet screen, so visit the table in the back and then come smile with me," Dana concluded waving as she left the podium.

The room gave her a standing ovation and mobbed the shelter table, while volunteers scurried to hand out applications and accept checks. People joined the shelter's mailing list, and the cameras clicked and flashed for an hour.

⚡ **21** ⚡

Elizabeth Johnson took the microphone and announced that the scavenger hunt participants should meet in the lobby next to the candy table in fifteen minutes. Thirty people joined her and received their reusable trick-or-treat bags, the scavenger hunt list, and instructions. The first five people back to this spot got to select any carved pumpkin on the property.

The sun was setting, giving the woods an orange glow. Once twilight set in, the low lights on the trail, graveyard, and maze created shadows, adding to the ambience of the festivities.

A fresh group of people arrived dressed as ghouls, zombies, and witches. Albert Holton led the way, wearing a simple outfit of black slacks and a black sweater. Without makeup or a real costume, his tousled dark brown hair and all black clothing made him look like a warlock leading a band of evil acolytes into the party.

People looked at them with some recognition, especially the famous director. He stopped to give autographs to those who asked and suggested they get signatures from his troupe of actors, who gladly signed notepads, napkins, and T-shirts handed to them by fans.

Several people approached one of the actors in her deluxe witch costume. Ward heard them remark how much they loved her hat adorned with black roses and how her magic wand looked real. She told them that the hat was custom made to her specifications as she posed for photos with fans.

Ward watched the woman keep score of how many signatures she gave compared to her fellow actors with a tic mark on her palm after signing for each fan.

"I wonder how many autographs Dana Wood signed today," said Susan out loud to no one in particular.

"Over a hundred, I'd say," said Ward.

Susan looked over at the pirate standing nearby.

"How do you know?"

"She gave away signed photographs and took pictures with people who donated to the shelter. A generous woman."

"Hmm," Susan pressed her lips together.

"Don't like her much?"

"What's it to you?"

97

"Watch yourself before you make more enemies than you can handle." The pirate glared at the witch with one eye.

Susan squinted her eyes and followed the rest of the actors inside.

È

A while after Chrissy heard the pounding of more feet across the floor, she came out from under the desk and shook out her hair. Her butterfly wings stayed in place despite the rigorous shaking.

Uncle Steve was busy talking with someone, and Mickey was being adored by the woman next to him. Chrissy ran under the velvet rope and up the stairs, her butterfly wings flapping wildly. She looked at Dana's door, which was closed. She looked at Gail's door, and saw it was slightly open, enough for her little fuzzy paw to push it open and have a look around. She saw the shoes near the closet and avoided those. She remembered what happened the last time she was in here.

She sniffed around the bathroom door and checked out the floor near the bed. The frame sat high enough that she could wiggle under it. That's when she saw a black flower. She pushed it and ducked low to see if it responded. Nothing. She pawed at it again. Sparkles dusted the floor. She sniffed at it and sneezed, scattering the glitter. Some landed on her head.

This room had too many things that made her sneeze. She exited the way she came, leaving the door open.

È

Gail brought Dana water and whisked her away to freshen up.

"Your speech was uplifting, heartfelt, and motivating. I'll bet they get enough money to run the shelter for the next two years," said Gail as they went up to their rooms.

"I hope so," said Dana.

Gail's door was open.

"Maybe we should get Ray," suggested Dana.

È

Autumn picked glitter from Chrissy's hair.

"What have you gotten yourself into?"

Chrissy's gaze intensified. Autumn put her head against Chrissy's forehead. The world spun to a lower point of view. She found herself under a bed, staring at a black rose with glitter on it. The world shifted back to normal when she pulled her head back.

Autumn discovered Chrissy's special gift of showing Autumn what she sees when they solved the case of Chrissy's first pet parent, Gary

Martin. Chrissy's extraordinary talent provided information they couldn't have gotten any other way.

"Whose bed were you under?"

Autumn's phone vibrated with a text from Gail asking to send Ray up. She found her door open.

"Is that where you were little one?"

Chrissy licked Autumn's cheek. Autumn covered her head with kisses.

The text she sent to Ray got him to come inside. He and Ace ascended the staircase to Gail's room. Autumn and Chrissy followed.

"The door was open," said Gail.

Ray looked around.

"Is anything missing or out of place?"

"Not that I can see. Just thought you'd want to know about it."

"I think I know how the door got pushed open," said Autumn holding Chrissy. "Don't let this sweet face fool you."

"How do you know she was up here?"

Autumn sometimes forgot she had to be careful about the information Chrissy shared. Ray was the only other person who knew of Chrissy's ability.

"Is there glitter in here?"

"I don't think so," said Gail.

"It would have to be on the floor for it to get on Chrissy's head."

Autumn bent down and looked under the bed. The rose lay in a small pile of glitter.

"There," she pointed to it and moved out of the way.

Ray pulled on a glove, kneeled down, and retrieved the black rose.

"Where did that come from?" asked Gail.

Dana shrugged.

"Do you remember locking the door?" asked Ray.

"I thought I did."

"It must have been partially open for Chrissy to get in here. Her body probably pushed it open all the way."

"But how did it get open in the first place?" Ray thought aloud. "I need a bag for this rose."

Autumn texted Kim to bring one up.

Kim asked, "What's going on?"

"Were you cleaning in here today?" asked Autumn.

"I didn't get a chance. Too much going on."

"Gail's door was open. Did you see anyone come up here?"

"No. But with all the people here today, you never know."

Ray bagged the rose and radioed an officer to come get it and take it to the lab.

Dana came downstairs to find Albert Holton and the crew dipping into the candy bowls.

"Hey! Glad you made it," said Dana.

"Where's Gail?" Albert asked.

"Upstairs, uh, freshening up. You guys look great," said Dana. "Have you checked out the vendors downstairs?"

"We're heading down now," one of the ghouls said.

"There's a bowling alley if anyone's interested, and lots of food vendors." said Dana.

Most of them headed to the basement. Susan DiMarco stayed near Albert.

"Hello, Susan."

"Dana." Susan said in a clipped tone.

"How are you holding up?" asked Albert, touching Dana's arm.

"As well as can be expected. Thanks for asking."

Albert guided her away from Susan and into the den.

Dana glimpsed Susan clench her fists, and with no invitation to join them, she followed the others downstairs.

"Do you need more time?"

Dana appreciated his concern.

"I'll be back on set Monday. There's something healing about this place. It's a different from LA."

Albert smiled.

"Why do you think I live here and not there?"

"I'm thinking of moving out here. Autumn connected me to a local realtor."

"Glad to hear it! I've got plenty of work for you." He squeezed her hands gently.

"I was hoping you'd say that."

㊘〶

Susan watched as the cast and crew went from booth to booth, chatting and laughing. They were so comfortable with each other. Why did she always feel like the outsider?

She stopped at the jewelry booth and tried on a silver necklace adorned with garnets. The price tag was reasonable, but she hadn't received a paycheck yet, so she put the necklace back on the stand and grabbed a card from the counter. She'd go back and get it on payday, if no one bought it today.

The cast was farther down the hallway in front of what looked like a bakery. She was trying to be likeable. She'd even apologized for her outburst on Wednesday. Despite that, the others avoided her. She wanted to be in on their inside jokes, not be the subject of them.

One of the ghouls looked up and saw her watching them. He waved her over. Maybe things were looking up.

૭৪

"Have you been through the trail yet?" asked Dana. "Talk about atmospheric."

Albert let her lead him outside to the trailhead. A uniformed officer nodded at them.

The tiny lights lit the area adequately to see the path and the statuary along the way. Scavenger hunt participants ran through, stopping when they discovered an item on the list and taking a square to prove it.

"They did an excellent job."

"Elizabeth Johnson conceptualized and installed the Halloween decorations. She's amazing."

"She certainly has a flair. I'll put her on the list of alternates for set decoration."

Dana smiled. Having it be Albert's idea was better than making a suggestion.

They stopped at the pond. The water glistened; the twinkle lights reflected on the calm surface. Something moved in the leaves. A witch peeked out from behind a tree, an uplight casting eerie shadows.

"I think I've found the location of my next film," Albert said, delighted. "This whole place lends itself to mysterious goings on."

"I'll introduce you to the owner."

૭৪

Hanging out with the cast bored Susan. She tried to understand their humor and why they cared about one another, but couldn't. She excused herself when they stopped at the bowling lanes and worked her way back toward the party upstairs.

Adults and children bobbed for apples, people drank warm apple cider with cinnamon sticks, and the constant click of cameras and flashes went off in the living room. Laughter floated in the air. A little dog with long hair came up to her.

"What do you want?"

The dog sniffed her leg.

101

"Get away from me!"

A woman came running over and grabbed the dog.

"Is everything okay?"

"Why is there a dog in a public place?" demanded Susan.

"I'm Autumn. I own this property. And this is my Shih Tzu, Chrissy. Did she hurt you?"

"No, she was sniffing me."

"I can see you're upset. Would you like some warm apple cider or hot chocolate?"

"No, just keep that dog away from me."

Susan stormed out the front door.

❧

Chrissy was unfazed by the outburst. She looked at Autumn and put her head against her mommy's. Autumn's balance dipped for a moment as Chrissy showed her the black rose once again. The world came back into focus. Chrissy had smelled Susan's scent on the rose.

❧

Julie Hall rushed over with Teddy cradled in the crook of her arm.

"Who was that?" said Julie, watching the woman stomp out the door.

"I think she's one of the cast members from Dana's movie."

"Well, she certainly isn't a good representative of the production."

❧

Dana led Albert through the hay bale maze and into the graveyard. They stood alone among the tombstones. Susan hid behind a tree, seething at their intimate friendship.

❧

A scream pierced the air.

"It's Dana Wood! She's hurt!" the woman yelled as she ran toward the house. "And there's a man lying on the ground. He's not moving!"

Ray, Ace, and Adam rushed to meet her.

"Where?" asked Ray.

"In the graveyard! She's covered in blood!"

"Stay here," Ray said to the woman. Then to Adam "Why wasn't anyone watching Dana?" as they ran to the graveyard.

"There are officers all over the place. I don't know how she slipped past them."

When they arrived, people gathered in the graveyard, taking pictures of the bodies while chattering excitedly.

"Is it really her?"

"Who's the guy?"

"What's that sticking out of her?"

"So much blood!"

"Please clear the area," said Ray, while Adam guided them away from the crime scene.

"Why is she tied up?"

Ray noticed that the rope holding Dana was the same Navy knot Ward Everly used on the hay bales.

"Please go back to the house," asked Adam.

Ray, Adam, and Ace formed a barrier that pushed back the gawkers, making them turn and walk toward the house. The three stayed with them until they reached the front door to the mansion and guided them in.

Autumn stood in the entryway holding Chrissy. She stepped to the side to let people into the mansion.

"What's going on?" she asked Ray.

"Looks like Dana and Albert were attacked."

"Oh, no!"

"Try to keep these people inside so we can figure out what happened."

Autumn waved Elizabeth over and asked her to announce the winners of the scavenger hunt.

"Have you seen Ward Everly?" asked Ray.

"Not lately."

The three officers went back to the cemetery. They found drag marks where Dana Wood and Albert Holton used to be. Their flashlights revealed a stripe of red in the groove of one of them.

☙

Ward Everly huffed and puffed as he pulled the bodies from their resting places. The rope made it easier to drag them out of the cemetery and through the bushes. He looked down at Dana, her costume now more red than white. The magic wand sticking out of her chest caused more red stuff to flow.

☙

Gail appeared holding a cup of cider and noticed the commotion in the lobby.

103

"What's going on?" she asked Autumn.

Autumn looked down, not wanting to be the one to tell her.

"It's Dana."

"What about her?"

"She and Albert were attacked in the graveyard."

"What?!"

Autumn took the cup from Gail's hand and put it on the table.

"Ray and Adam are out there right now."

Autumn's cell vibrated with a text message. She took a moment to read it and let it sink in.

Gail wrung her hands and paced.

"Ray says the bodies are gone. It looks like someone dragged them off."

Gail's eyes opened wide.

"I want to see what's happening," said Gail.

"Ray asked everyone to stay in here. He'll give us an update as soon as he knows anything."

"I'm going to my room. Call me on my cell with any news."

⋈

Adam gathered those with photos of the crime scene in the den. He studied them all, hoping for clues. He sent the clearest shots to his phone. He saw the eighteen-inch wood wand poking out from Dana's chest. He had seen the witch's wand at some point during the festivities, but with so many witches running around here, it was anybody's guess which witch it belonged to.

He wondered why dead bodies showed up at Knollwood festivities, like at the Peabody Festival a few months back. Other than that, Knollwood was a quiet town.

⋈

Ray and Ace followed the drag marks and the shoe prints through the bushes. The ground looked trampled, disturbed by several sets of footprints. Red droplets dotted the churned earth, and the wooden magic wand lay red and slick on the ground.

Ace sniffed the area, and the wand, then followed the scent farther into the woods. Ray used his flashlight to follow the tracks and broken branches. Ace tugged at his restraint and pulled Ray out to the dead-end road, where he lost the trail.

Night had fully fallen. With no street lamps at the end of the road, the darkness was dense, broken only by the lights from the mansion up ahead. Ray radioed his officer down at the museum and asked if a car had passed from the direction of the dead end. The answer was no. Ray scratched his head and walked Ace back to the mansion.

⊰⊱

Autumn ran over to them, Chrissy bouncing in her arms.
"Did you find her?"
Ray shook his head, no.
She held Chrissy close, trying to comfort herself.
"Did Ward turn up?"
"I saw him in the dining room a few minutes ago."
"Did you notice his shoes?"
"What about them?"
"Were they caked with dirt?"
"I didn't notice."
Ray led Ace into the house and toward the dining room. Ward was there drinking hot chocolate with mini marshmallows and chatting with Maureen Roberts. Ray looked at his shoes. No caked dirt.
There was no reaction from Ace.
Adam came from the den over to Ray.
"Anything useful in the photos?"
"I got a good look at the wand and the knot, but that's it. It was too dark."
"Do you have an evidence bag? I need to bag the wand."
Adam pulled one from his vest and handed it to Ray.
"I'll be right back."
Ray walked Ace back to where they saw the wand. No sound came from the surrounding woods. The wand was still there. Ray pulled on a rubber glove and bagged the dripping wand. Something didn't feel right about any of this.

⊰⊱

The buzz inside the mansion was that Dana Wood's murderer was likely still on the grounds. Rather than being put off by the possibility of running into him or her, guests hung out and continued to enjoy everything the event offered. They also wanted to stay in case anything else happened.
Autumn and her friends sat in the living room apart from the guests. Chrissy, Mickey, Teddy, and Clay played together nearby, unaware of Dana's disappearance.
Gail entered the room, no longer wearing her sunflower costume.

105

"I found the cast and crew downstairs and let them know the situation," she said.

"Do you think one of them might be the culprit?" asked Stephanie.

"Why would they hurt the star and the director? Wouldn't that be bad for them? It would shut down the production," said Steve.

"That's a good point," Julie agreed.

Her husband, Brad, nodded his agreement.

"What if they hurt her and then kidnapped her? They might call with a ransom request," offered Beatrice.

Jasper sat beside her, patting her hand.

They heard a murmur in the crowd outside the living room that rose so they could hear it.

"I'm telling you I just saw her."

"I did, too. She was on the trail, looking at me from the shadows."

"I saw her dress covered in blood."

"Her ghost is haunting the woods."

"Can you guys stay here and watch Chrissy?" asked Autumn.

"Sure," said Stephanie.

But the moment Autumn moved toward the door, Chrissy was on her heels. Autumn gave in and scooped her up. She spotted Adam and waved him over.

"Can you radio Ray and tell him people saw Dana in the woods?"

Adam reached for his mic as he followed Autumn out the door.

People milled about outside, laughter came from the maze, and loud voices drifted in the air from the trails. The movie cast and crew stood in a circle wondering what to do. Susan DiMarco stood just outside of their group.

Ray and Ace met them at the trailhead and put his arm up, blocking Autumn from going in.

"Stay here," he ordered.

"Ray, check it out," Autumn subtly pointed towards Susan. "Her hat has black roses on it."

Adam chimed in, "She had a wand earlier, but I don't see it now."

"Adam, have our officer inside escort her to one of the empty guest rooms and hold her until we get back," instructed Ray.

Adam called the officer standing watch at the basement door to come get Susan. He stayed and watched Susan yelling and trying to pull away from the policeman. He whispered something to her that encouraged her to go with him.

Ward Everly stood at the doorway and gazed at Susan with a knowing smirk. Susan sneered at him as she walked past.

Ace put his nose down as they entered the woodland path. With all the people traipsing through here, Ray doubted he'd pick up Dana's scent.

Someone in the crowd called to Ray, "Doing a little ghost hunting?" followed by laughter.

"I don't believe in ghosts," he said, pulling his flashlight from his belt.

Adam walked cautiously behind him, looking left to right with his own flashlight, pushing away the shadows that obstructed his view.

The scarecrows and witches Elizabeth strategically placed in the woods distracted them. Movement to the right caught Ace's attention, and he yanked Ray off the path and into the trees. Adam followed. A flash of white farther down the trail sent visitors screaming and running. Ace changed course, while Adam continued in the same direction.

The screaming visitors cleared the trail, allowing Ray to run behind Ace at full speed. Another glimpse of white among the trees, closer now. Suddenly, a form stepped onto the trail, making them skid to a stop.

Leaves rustling and crunching to their right delivered Adam onto the trail, holding Albert Holton's arm.

Dana laughed. Ace smelled the fake blood and sat in front of her.

"Good boy!" said Dana.

Ray bent over, hands on his knees, to catch his breath.

"You guys really had us worried," he said.

"No wonder people were screaming," said Adam. "You look wicked with all that fake blood."

"It was a prank to promote the film," said Albert, brushing leaves from his sweater. Then to Adam, "You didn't have to tackle me."

Adam grinned. "After what you put us through, you deserved it."

"Touché," Albert agreed.

"Let's get inside and show folks you're neither dead nor a ghost," said Ray.

⋐⋑

Party guests exclaimed in surprise and excitement as Dana Wood and Albert Holton came through the door ahead of two police officers.

"Who's going to see *Dark Hollow Road* when it comes out?" yelled Albert.

107

Thunderous applause ensued as Dana took a bow and Albert clapped her on the back, pulling his hand away covered in sticky fake blood.

Gail came out of the living room, clapping for their performance, followed by Autumn and her friends. The reporters she called and asked to keep a low profile snapped photos and interviewed Dana and Albert to get the whole story.

Autumn looked on in shock and relief. The audience in the lobby smiled and giggled with delight at being present for the reveal. The cast and crew had wide, knowing grins. Ward leaned against the wall with his arms crossed, smiling ear to ear.

"Scary, eh?" said Gail.

"I'll say," Autumn said, letting out the breath she didn't know she held. "You could have let me in on it."

"Couldn't. I needed you to react authentically, scared for Dana's wellbeing."

"You got me! You deserve an Academy Award. My reaction was definitely heartfelt...and heart pounding!"

"See that ghoul with the pink hair in the group of crew members? She's the special effects supervisor. She did the makeup on Dana. Convincing, right?"

The ghoul looked their way, smiled, and wiggled her fingers.

Autumn waved back, shaking her head.

She looked over at Ray, who pointed upstairs and left to talk to Susan DiMarco.

"Where's he going?" asked Gail.

"To talk to Susan. Did you notice that her hat has black roses on it covered in glitter?"

"What was she doing in my room?"

"Ray's going to find out."

Kim stood nearby listening to their conversation and thanking goodness she didn't say anything about the note she'd found in Gail's room when they first arrived. Now it all made sense.

 C3 80

Susan sat on a chair scowling at the officer standing by the door when Ray walked in. He dismissed the officer and sat on the loveseat near Susan.

"What was all that noise downstairs?"

"We found Dana and Albert."

"You mean they're not dead?"

"Nope. It was a prank. You didn't know?"

Susan looked down and shook her head.

"They didn't let me in on the joke."

"Aren't you part of the cast? They all seemed to know about it."

"I'm from Hollywood. These guys are local. I'm not one of them, so they don't tell me anything."

"Gail is from Hollywood, too, isn't she?"

"Yeah."

"She was in on it. In fact, I think she orchestrated the whole thing as a publicity stunt."

"Wouldn't put it past her. She's known for pulling out all the stops for her clients."

"She's not your publicist, is she?"

"No."

"Then what were you doing in her room?"

"I, I, wanted to know what was upstairs. I wanted to see Dana's room compared to what they gave me in town. It was the only door that was unlocked," Susan stammered.

"Whose room did you think it was?"

"I hoped it was Dana's, but wasn't sure."

"Is this yours?" Ray held up the wooden magic wand.

"Yes."

"Someone used it as a prop for Dana's death scene."

"I must have put it down someplace and one of the crew picked it up and put it there."

"You're lucky it was staged and not for real."

Susan was quiet.

"How did you know I was in here?"

"The black rose you left behind."

⊂₰⊃

Ward watched Susan come down the stairs, pale and pouting. Ray came down behind her. Ward waited for Ray to pass by, then whispered to Susan, "Watch where you leave your things. They could get you into trouble."

"Look who's talking," Susan said, defiantly, and went outside.

⊂₰⊃

Dana peeled off the ruined gown and put it in a trash bag. Stage blood ruined clothing because of its sticky consistency. She showered off the mixture of corn syrup and red dye feeling immediately refreshed. She

109

donned jeans, her favorite cable-knit sweater, and ankle boots, put on some makeup, and rejoined the party.

Another round of applause accompanied her trip down the staircase.

Kim Stokes stood at the bottom of the stairs waiting for Dana.

"Hi, Dana!" said Kim, excitedly.

"Hi, Kim," replied Dana. "Nice to see you."

"I want you to meet my sister, Hannah."

Dana extended her hand. The young girl looked in her mid-teens. Her honey-brown skin and black hair were in sharp contrast to Kim's pale skin and blue eyes.

Hannah saw the confusion on Dana's face.

"I'm adopted."

Dana swallowed. "Do you live close by?"

"No, I live in Easton. Kim came and got me. I'm such a huge fan."

"Thank you. I'm always honored to meet a fan."

Dana wondered, then pushed the thought aside, and wondered again. Could it be her? Could it be her baby?

"I've seen all of your movies," Hannah declared.

"I appreciate that. How old are you?"

"Fourteen."

That's the right age.

"When is your birthday?"

"Valentine's Day," Hannah said.

Dana's gut shook.

"I'll get tickets for both of you to see the film I just finished shooting in Scotland. It's coming out around Christmas."

"That's great!" exclaimed Kim.

"And since I'm staying for the next few months to film in New Hope, maybe you two can come on the set after school. Bring your parents."

Kim and Hannah jumped up and down.

"This is amazing!" said Hannah.

You have no idea, thought Dana.

≈ 22 ≈

The last of the partiers left around midnight. The vendors in the basement loudly packed up. As Autumn walked through holding Chrissy, they told her the event made their whole financial month and wanted to be on the list for the next time.

"I can't believe how many books I sold today!" said Stacey. "Do you mind if I pack the rest up tomorrow? This little guy is pooped." She pointed to Clay snoring in his haunted house.

"Of course. I also found a ton of books in the attic I'd like you to appraise when you get time."

Stacey rubbed her hands together. "That's my favorite thing."

"See you tomorrow," Autumn waved and walked to Lisa's empty booth.

"You packed up fast," said Autumn.

"Nothing to pack. I sold everything."

"Wow, good for you. I don't think there are any of your cards left on the table upstairs. Come to think of it, there are no business cards at all."

"Did you talk to Sarah Kelly?"

"No. It was too hectic with the almost murder and kidnapping." They laughed.

"I'll talk to her next week once we get the place back in order."

"I'll let her know you'll call."

Autumn went back to the main floor and closed the basement door to block the noise. Those with booths near the main entrance had already broken down their booths. The rest exited toward the other end of the basement.

Ray and Ace played with Chrissy in the den. Autumn plopped herself onto the sofa, exhausted.

"The mini murder mystery was unexpected," said Ray.

"While it was entertaining for the guests, it scared me to death."

"I got a hint they'd staged it when the blood-soaked wand was dripping and gave off a faint scent of sugar. I'm pretty sure that's what Ace smelled and followed."

"Good boy," said Autumn, rubbing Ace's head.

"No wonder Ward was acting strangely. He was in on it."

"I still think there's something else going on with him, but I'm too tired to figure it out right now."

Chrissy jumped up on the sofa next to her mommy. Autumn lifted her up, covered her with kisses, and sat Chrissy down next to her.

Ray listened to the quiet.

"Where is everyone?"

"I sent Kim and Elizabeth home. They wanted to stay and start cleaning up, but we can do that on Monday. I'll do what I can tomorrow."

She leaned against Ray with Chrissy between them.

"You did a wonderful job," Ray said, and kissed her forehead.

"It was a group effort."

"Where are Dana and Gail?"

"In their rooms. They were too tired for evening tea. Now that the prank is over, Gail said she's flying back to Los Angeles on Monday."

"Dana's staying through December, right?"

"Longer than that. I introduced her to Maureen. They're going house hunting next weekend."

"I'm sure she'll get more for her money in Upper Bucks County than she does in Beverly Hills."

"I'm glad she's staying. She fits right in. She's more relaxed than when she first got here."

೮౩೮

Dana sat in her room thinking about Hannah. The girl had an easy smile and exuberant energy. She saw herself and the father in her lovely face. She could see that the girl was loved and in a supportive home environment, something Dana could not give her. The travel, the spotlight, the gossip did not create a normal life for a teenager.

As much as Dana wanted to reveal that she was the biological mother, the disruption it would cause wasn't worth it. She loved her child too much to put her through that. Dana wanted Hannah to thrive and have a stable home life. The tabloids would have a field day, and would likely discover the senator's paternity.

Without a DNA test, she couldn't prove that Hannah was hers, but her heart knew that this was the baby she had to give up all those years ago. Now she had a face and a name. She could develop a friendship with her in a way that they could have fun together without stirring up a difficult history. Dana could include Hannah's parents to make them feel at ease and provide financial support if they need it.

Moving to the area gave her more opportunities to keep track of Hannah's progress. Getting to know Kim was a bonus. Knowing Autumn, Ray, Stephanie, Adam, Lisa, and Elizabeth gave her a head start to plant roots in the community. They were genuinely kind people she trusted not to take advantage of her fame. They had her back when they thought she was in harm's way. She felt safe around them.

Dana smiled thinking about house hunting with Maureen and opened her computer to a real estate website to make a list of places she wanted to see.

≠ **23** ≠

Dana had already left for the set by the time Autumn and Kim helped Gail bring her bags down by way of the elevator. The limo driver and his assistant loaded them into the car.

"This has been so much fun," said Gail. "I enjoyed my stay immensely and plan to tell everyone in my circle and on social media."

"That's fabulous! Thank you!" said Autumn. The mental image of the inn full year round made her heart flutter.

They hugged.

"I'll keep in touch," Gail waved as she got into the limo.

Kim and Autumn waved back.

"No wonder that room was so jammed. She had five suitcases of clothes. That's more than I have in my closet," said Kim.

"Now you can clean it the way you like," said Autumn, thinking of Kim's frustration at tip-toeing around the piles of clothing and cosmetics in Gail's room.

"I'm going in! I'll see you in a few hours."

She enthusiastically grabbed her cart and took the elevator back up.

Chrissy charged through the lobby into the den and then charged from the den to the living room and back again, reclaiming her space.

They cleaned up the common areas, except for the decorations that Elizabeth worked to transition into Thanksgiving. The mansion was far down the road and unlikely to have trick-or-treaters on Halloween, which was two weeks away, so she took some woodland witches, scarecrows, and ghosts into attic storage and the rest to Autumn's primary residence where trick-or-treaters were more likely to go. She and Kim had fun cleaning and organizing the attic storage space to make it easier for next year's Halloween season.

The pumpkins carved by Stephanie's students were a hit, and the scavenger hunt winners got first pick. They held back a few to bring to Autumn's house and gave the rest to guests to bring home. For the mansion, Elizabeth replaced them with gourds and uncarved pumpkins so they'd last through the season.

She also took down the photo backdrop and stored it upstairs until Autumn opened for business. Then they'd find a permanent spot for it, probably in the lobby.

The floor cleaners pulled up in a van and unloaded the equipment to scrub and polish the slate floors to go from grimy to gleaming.

Autumn let them in and then gathered up Chrissy and dressed her for a walk. She needed quiet, not more noise.

She waved to Ward Everly, who was dismantling the hay bale maze. Autumn donated the hay bales to the owner of Appleworth's farm, who was expected to pick them up in the morning.

The fall air was crisp, with the scent of wet leaves. The breeze dislodged leaves that rained over the pair as they enjoyed the solitude of the woodland trail. It was nice to have the place to themselves. Chrissy trotted ahead, her body swaying, looking for something to sniff.

Elizabeth had removed the baskets of tokens from the scavenger hunt, but the twinkle lights and battery-operated tea lights remained. Those provided a magical sparkle all year round.

Chrissy stopped and pawed the ground.

"What is it, sweetheart?"

She dug at the damp leaves with her front paws. The tip of a piece of paper emerged. Autumn pulled out the moist and slightly smeared newspaper clipping.

The headline read: *La Jolla Handyman Suspected in Death of Amy Davis*. In regard to the ongoing investigation of Amy Davis' death, police interviewed Alice Crocker, the former girlfriend of Ward Everly. Crocker found several drafts of threatening letters he wrote to Amy Davis similar to the one Davis' aunt, Zelda Weems, turned into detectives. Crocker indicated that the letter was likely the result of Ward Everly's obsession with Dana Wood. Police want Everly for questioning. Those with information, please contact Detective Connors at the Los Angeles police department.

Cut from what looked like the center of the page, there was no date and no indication of which publication it came from.

Chrissy looked up at her and wagged her tail.

"You're such a smart girl!"

Chrissy smiled. Autumn dialed Ray.

ભ્ઠ

Ray pulled into the mansion's driveway with Ace secured in the backseat. Ward worked on untying the last of the hay bales. Adam pulled in behind Ward's red work truck.

Ward looked up. "How are you fellas doing?"

"Just fine, Ward," said Ray.

He pulled up a photo on his phone and showed it to Ward.

"Any idea why the Los Angeles police want to talk to you?"

Ward read the clipping.

"Alice always was a big mouth. That's why I cut her loose."

"That doesn't answer his question," said Adam.

"Probably because I sent Amy Davis a letter to scare her off from her affair with Michael Williams. Dana Wood is too nice a person to have the likes of Amy Davis interfering in her life."

"Did you kill her?"

"Heck, no. I was long gone by then. I sent that letter just before I moved here six months ago."

"We'll need to take you to the station and call Detective Connors in L.A. so you can tell him your side of it. It should be easy to verify your story."

"Sure is."

"Anything else you want to say?" asked Ray.

"Yeah, did Dana ever get the stuffed bear I bought for her?"

Ray and Adam looked at each other.

"That was from you?"

"I dropped it off after I finished a job. It was late, and the lights were off, so I left it on the porch."

Ray shook his head. Taken for a ride twice in two weeks.

"Why didn't you sign the note?"

"It was kind of embarrassing to admit how I feel about her, so I let it be anonymous."

"We'll make sure she gets it."

"Tell her it's from me. She's used to having me around now, so she might be okay with accepting my gift."

"You can tell her. Let's go."

With Ward loaded into the back seat of Adam's police car, Ray went to talk to Autumn, who watched the scene unfold from behind the curtains. She opened the door to greet him with Chrissy at her side.

"At least we know what felt off about him," said Autumn.

"He also admitted to leaving the stuffed bear on the front steps."

"That's a two-for-one bonus gift."

"I don't think he's a murderer. He felt it was his duty to protect Dana. He'll be in the clear by later today."

"Good. His skills are excellent. I'd hate to lose him."

"Going forward, he better let the police and Dana's bodyguards protect her."

"I think he was more concerned about her reputation, not physical harm."

"As long as she stays here, she's our responsibility."

"The entire town knows she's staying here."

"My men are taking overnight shifts, and I'll be on the inside with Ace, so we have it covered."

Chrissy barked once and wagged her tail.

"I didn't forget about you, my little detective. You'll protect her, too," said Ray, rubbing her head.

Dana sat in her trailer waiting for her next scene. It was only a few days ago that Gail had left, and she missed her presence. It was fun staying with her at the inn and planning that gag. She sent a text to Gail with an update that the police confirmed Ward Everly had nothing to do with Amy Davis' murder and telling her how cute the stuffed bear was. She also teased her with how delicious last night's dinner was with Lisa Coleman's special pasta with white clam sauce and freshly baked bread.

Gail texted back how much she missed Lisa's cooking, and then dropped a bombshell. The investigation of Amy Davis' death now extended to Michael. The authorities didn't think it was suicide. She wasn't sure of the details, but the rumor mill was churning out speculation around both deaths.

Dana put the phone down and wondered what Michael had gotten himself into. She was glad to be in Pennsylvania and not Southern California. The only gossip she wanted to hear was about the goat on Appleworth's farm breaking through the fence to eat the neighbor's favorite butterfly bush.

She felt safe here, except for her daily exposure to the toxic Susan DiMarco. The casting director wanted to send her home, but Mel Argento must have something on him, because Susan got to stay. There was a part of Dana that felt sorry for Susan and another part feeling like Susan brought it on herself. Either way, Dana avoided her when possible, as did the rest of the cast and crew.

Word spread that she went into Gail's room and left evidence of the intrusion. They held Gail Armstrong in high regard, so looked down about Susan's invasion of privacy. The movie industry was a close community whose tentacles reached far beyond Hollywood. Word spread quickly of actors who displayed distasteful behavior. This might be Susan's last movie role, but her future selling household cleaners and fast food in television commercials looked promising.

ଔ୫ଓ

Susan saw Dana emerge from her trailer refreshed and camera ready while Susan was sweating from the heavy makeup and prosthetics her character required. She hadn't had a break since the two-hour makeup session early that morning. Her first inclination was to complain and snap at people, but stuffed it down.

Ever since her explosive arrival on set last week, Susan had become a pariah. No one spoke to her during lunch, so she took to having lunch in the woods. They chose someone else to be Dana's understudy, destroying her plans to rise in Albert Holton's eyes. That's when she knew her only chance to reach Dana's level of fame required her to stand out another way.

She heard of Method actors who went so deep into their characters that they lost themselves. These actors had a notorious reputation for being difficult to work with. Susan had a head start in that department. It was time to connect her naturally foul moods to creative genius rather than the perception of Susan as uncooperative and angry. She would become the creature.

☙

Kim and Hannah Stokes arrived on the set of *Dark Hollow Road*, giddy and smiling. Dana was in the middle of a scene, so the production manager led them to a seating area where they could watch. He put his finger to his lips, and they nodded.

The cameras, people holding clipboards, the large microphones, and lighting fascinated them and added to the excitement. The creatures coming out of the woods made Kim think of The Peabody Mansion trails and how Elizabeth expertly cloaked the witches and scarecrows within the trees.

No sooner had she thought of Elizabeth, than she appeared from behind the large camera holding a clipboard. She made notes and checked a thick pile of papers that Kim assumed was the script. She silently waved.

Elizabeth looked up and smiled, waving back. She put a finger to her lips. Kim nodded.

The director yelled cut, and everyone relaxed, speaking in low tones. Elizabeth bounced over to them.

"Hi, ladies!"

"Since when do you work here?" asked Kim.

"Dana showed Mr. Holton my trail design. After he experienced the cemetery, he contacted me as an extra hand for the set decoration department. I'm learning so much." Elizabeth's eyes shone with excitement.

Dana walked over to them.

"Having fun?"

119

"This is great!" said Hannah.

Kim agreed.

"Anybody thirsty? I have water in my trailer."

Dana gestured for them to follow her.

"Wow, a real movie star trailer," said Hannah.

Dana laughed and pulled bottled water from the mini refrigerator.

"Who's that?" asked Kim, looking out the window.

Dana and Elizabeth both went to look. A creature stood staring at the trailer, moving stiffly as coaches instructed them to do during filming.

"That's Susan DiMarco," said Dana. "She was at the Halloween Extravaganza."

"Right, I remember now. She broke into Gail's room to look around," said Kim. "I think Gail locked the door out of habit. I've seen her do it."

"Why is she moving like that? And she's staring right at us," said Hannah.

"I'm not sure," said Dana. "I have to get back. Come with me and stay near the crew."

Kim watched Dana lock the trailer door.

"Afraid she'll break into your room, too?"

"I like being careful," said Dana diplomatically.

Kim saw the creature hold up her clawed hands, point a long nail at Dana, and skulk away.

"She's weird. What's her problem?"

"Maybe she's practicing her moves for a scene," Dana answered.

"I don't think she likes you," Hannah observed.

⊂ॐ⊃

Ward Everly stood behind a trailer in the lot, watching Susan DiMarco acting crazy. He didn't like the way she threatened Dana and planned to put a stop to it. The security guards on set seemed lax in their duties, not recognizing the potential threats around Dana. If Ward was younger, he'd apply for the job, but even though he was in good shape at forty-three, it was unlikely they'd consider him.

Ray told him that they would take care of Dana's protection when she was at the mansion. No one said he couldn't watch her when she was at work.

He trailed Susan from a distance. He'd approach her when she took lunch alone in the woods.

≠ **25** ≠

Ray hit speed dial to get Autumn.

"Hi, Honey," she answered.

"You can call me honey, or you can call me Lieutenant Reed!"

"I'm so proud of you! Congratulations!"

"Everyone shook my hand, even the other candidates. It's great going into the job with so much support."

"They know you'll do right by them and have an ear to listen when there's an issue."

"A bunch of us are going to Hannigan's Bar to celebrate tonight. Mind if I drop off Ace before I head out?"

"Not at all. Chrissy will be thrilled. And he's the next best protector we have besides you."

"An officer will still be outside until I get there."

"That's fine. See you soon."

🙰

Sarah Kelly arrived on time for her interview wearing a white blouse with black slacks. She spun her long blonde hair into a twist. It looked like she was ready to start cooking. Autumn wondered what was in the large thermal bag that hung from her shoulder.

After Sarah met Chrissy, Autumn put her on the sofa in the den with a soft blanket and her favorite stuffed lamb toy that was as big as Chrissy herself.

"Stay here, sweetheart. We won't be long."

They went into the kitchen.

"This is beautiful. The layout is perfect to make multi-course meals," Sarah said.

"Tell me about the things you like to cook. What's your specialty?"

"My training includes everything from meat, chicken, and fish to full vegan meals. I also bake. Soups are my specialty and they vary by season. For fall, I'd make Carrot soup with miso, ginger, coconut, and orange."

"That sounds delicious."

"Try it for yourself." Sarah reached in the bag and lifted a container of orange-colored soup.

121

Autumn poured it into two cups and handed Sarah a spoon. The soup was smooth and rich.

"Mmm," said Autumn, nodding her head. "So good."

"Thank you."

"Did Lisa tell you we're not officially open yet, but we do have one very special guest?"

"Dana Wood, right?"

"Yes. She leaves early, and I can take care of breakfast. She gets back late, but enjoys a light supper. She'd enjoy this soup with fresh bread. She liked Lisa's pot pies, too. On weekends it would be breakfast and dinner."

"I can handle that."

"Are you open to working a part-time schedule until we have more guests?"

"That works well, since Lisa hired me part time at the café."

Autumn extended her hand.

"Welcome aboard!"

She showed Sarah out and went into the den to check on Chrissy. Her big dark eyes glistened in the dim light. Snuggled into the blanket, she rested her head on the stuffed lamb's neck.

"There's my beautiful baby. You're such a good girl."

♋

It was after ten o'clock when they heard the bang. It sounded like a gunshot, but the sound echoing through the woods could disguise the actual source of the noise. Ray still wasn't home. Autumn told Dana to lock herself in her room and stay away from the windows. She held Chrissy, shaking from the loud noise, safely in her arms.

Ace stood facing the wooded side of the house, hair bristling, his low growl enough to scare the pants off of any intruder. Autumn hoped it wouldn't come to that.

The officer guarding the outside of the house knocked on the door and identified himself as Charlie Osgood. Ace ran toward the door, his alert stance prepared for whatever came next. Autumn recognized Charlie's voice and opened the door.

Ace's growl intensified as he spotted movement in the woods on the periphery of the property. He took off, barking fiercely as the sound of running through leaves reached them. It was no small animal. A narrow penlight beam turned on to light the forest floor, but not enough to identify the runner. It clicked off again.

Charlie ran after Ace, clicking on his powerful flashlight beam. The light caught the back of a figure in black, but he couldn't see the full outline of the interloper. He was impossible to identify. A moving shadow and nothing more.

Ace no longer barked. Charlie only heard his own footfalls. Then out of the night, a deep growl and the sound of someone falling, followed by a ripping noise, scuffling, and more running.

"Ace! Come here, boy! C'mon!" called Charlie.

If the perpetrator had a weapon, he could hurt Ace, and he'd never forgive himself. Plus, Ray would have his head. The dog wore no protective gear, so a gun or knife would be fatal. He knew Ace would keep chasing after the trespasser until he pinned him to the ground.

Charlie had seen Ace's work in the field, a criminal on the ground as Ace snarled over them, revealing saliva-slick, long, white teeth. If the perpetrator had any sense, he stayed still beneath Ace's powerful body and terrifying teeth.

Ace strode out of the woods, heated from the chase, and a piece of black cloth in his mouth.

"Good boy! Atta boy!"

He pulled the fabric from Ace's mouth and dropped it into an evidence bag.

Ace panted from the exertion.

Autumn stood at the door, and Chrissy ran toward her friend. She barked at Charlie.

"You want to smell this?" He lowered the open bag so Chrissy could have a sniff, then sealed the bag.

"Ace, let's get you a drink of water," said Autumn. "C'mon Chrissy! You, too, Charlie."

Autumn filled Ace's large stainless-steel bowl with filtered water and put it in front of him. He took big laps, drinking three quarters of it before he stopped, then sunk to the cool tile floor to rest. Chrissy came over and sat next to her friend.

Charlie drank a glass of cold water while on the phone with Ray. Running like that made him realize he was out of shape and needed to jog regularly.

Autumn and Dana sat in the den where the windows were smaller and the curtains heavier. Autumn poured a couple fingers of scotch for each of them.

"He'll be here in about fifteen minutes," Charlie reported. "I'll wait outside for him."

⚡ **26** ⚡

Saturday's weather was perfect for house hunting. Maureen Roberts knew the area and the pros and cons of each property on the market. Today, she focused on three properties worthy of a buyer like Dana Wood. The criteria included privacy, woods, water, space for entertaining, multiple garages, and separate quarters for overnight guests. Every house on the tour offered these and more, but Maureen needed to see which architectural style Dana responded to, so she selected a contemporary, traditional stone colonial, and a French Normandy.

"I can't believe what two million dollars buys out here. I put my house in Beverly Hills on the market for eighteen million, and it sold in a week, furniture and all. These houses are as big or bigger than mine."

Professional packers gathered Dana's belongings, which were on a truck heading east.

"Don't forget the acreage. We have homes in the area closer to eighteen, if you prefer."

"Not when I can get what I need for less."

Dana knew she was home when they entered the gated driveway of a private estate on ten wooded acres in Knollwood. The stone home exuded casual elegance and gave her everything she wanted for herself and her guests within the nine thousand square foot layout. A two-acre pond with a dock and screened gazebo provided a calm place for Dana to do tai chi and read. The curved staircase in the grand foyer reminded her of The Peabody Mansion design she loved so much.

Dana pictured a personal chef in the huge gourmet kitchen and having Albert and her friends over to watch movies in the well-appointed theater room. A massive bar and floor-to-ceiling fireplace was perfect for intimate gatherings in the cooler months. Dana loved the brown leather overstuffed seating. The pool area and cabana provided a luxurious outdoor space to entertain in the summer.

The walk-in closet looked more like a retail store display with cherry cabinetry and shoe racks. The house had views of the Delaware River from the slate patio with an outdoor kitchen.

The carriage house with four garages and an apartment above filled her need for a guest space.

"This is the one. Let's put in an offer today that includes the furniture."

The high-end designer furniture throughout the house had the earthy, Pennsylvania feel Dana wanted. Her house in California had formal, glitzy décor that no longer suited her taste.

Maureen pulled up a contract on her tablet, and Dana used her finger to sign it before it zipped across cyberspace and to the homeowner's realtor.

The owners were eager to sell, and it was a cash purchase, so Maureen scheduled closing for the following Friday afternoon.

⚮

Dana told Autumn all about her new home over lunch. Autumn's excitement matched Dana's.

"I'm so happy for you, really," she told Dana. "I am going to miss you, though."

"No, you're not. You and Chrissy can come to my house. Ray and Ace are welcome, too."

"You're close to the inn and to my house down the street from Lisa, Steve, Mickey, Julie, Brad, and Teddy. I have backyard gatherings where the pups run around and everybody hangs out."

"I like having a built-in social life that doesn't include clubs or Hollywood hangouts. Being myself with people I trust is more relaxing."

"You won't miss being with people in your industry?"

"Albert Holton lives in the area. There are many others in Philadelphia and New York City. Some I know and some I'll get to know."

Chrissy pawed her leg.

"And you, little one," Dana said, lifting Chrissy into her lap, "You and that sweet face are forever part of my inner circle. Maybe we'll make a movie about you one day."

"She's already a diva. I'm not sure how much more I can take."

The conversation got quiet, both women thinking about the pending changes.

"The house has a special security system that includes cameras and a panic room."

"Let's hope you'll never have occasion to use it."

"Right."

"To be on the safe side, don't tell people about the new house. We still don't know who was running through the woods."

"If they think I'm still here, won't that put you at risk?"

"Not at all. Chrissy and I are going home when you move into your new place. Besides, it's been quiet since then."

"True."

"I'll ask Ray if we can trick people into thinking you're still here. You know, light timers, an officer stationed outside. He'll know what to do."

枅

Autumn broke the news to Ray about Dana leaving the inn the following weekend and floated her idea by him.

"I can always stay there with Ace. That way we can keep an eye out."

"Not alone. Chrissy and I can stay with you."

"No. You two go home. I'll get Adam to stay with me."

"My new chef, Sarah, can practice on the two of you for breakfast and dinner."

"We'll give Sarah an honest review, but heed this warning. You'll never get Adam out of there."

"I'll sic Stephanie on him if it comes to that."

枅

The analysis of the fabric Ace tore from the mystery runner showed an opaque blend of spandex, polyester, and nylon. This stretch fabric combination was common to both men's and women's attire, so didn't help Ray determine the gender of the trespasser. It did, however, give Ace something to track. He had the scent from his encounter. The fabric would remind him of the one that got away.

枅

In Los Angeles, Detective Connors reviewed the evidence pulled from Michael Williams' study. A judge gave police a last sweep of the room before the new buyers closed down access. The plastic bags on his desk held the clothes Michael wore when they found the body. Dana Wood donated the rest of his wardrobe to a local homeless shelter.

The problems between Michael and Dana briefly put her on Connors' radar as a possible suspect. Her travel documentation and constant accompaniment by her entourage gave her the most conclusive alibis for both deaths he had ever seen.

It was Michael, not Dana, the evidence tied to both his own and Amy's murder. The detective considered that if Michael killed Amy, his overwhelming grief at what he had done led him to commit suicide. But what if he hadn't killed her?

His motive to end his life would be that Dana Wood told him to move out and the divorce proceedings made public. The destruction of his reputation in Hollywood between his underhanded business deals and as a murder suspect in the Amy Davis case might also be motive.

The guy's life as he knew it was over, anyway. But photos of the body and the medical examiner's report showed blunt force trauma to Michael's head, similar to the injuries he sustained in the park but more recent. The gunshot wound occurred after the head injury. Based on the amount of blood, Michael was likely dead prior to being shot.

When he first interviewed Michael, Connors saw notes from the medical exam describing a head injury beyond falling over and landing on the ground. It was more like someone hit him with a heavy object, like a rock or bat. That would put another person at the scene.

Zelda Weems was odd and unable to provide an alibi, so she wasn't completely off his list. As Amy's sole heir, she had a motive. She also owned a bat that she regularly carried for self-defense.

Then he had Ward Everly, Dana's self-appointed protector. The letters he wrote threatening Amy weren't proof that he killed her. Besides, he'd sent that months ago and moved to Pennsylvania before her death.

Dana Wood got the text from Michael on Wednesday. Ken Blanchard found Michael Wednesday evening. Dana requested he check on Michael, worried that her rejection could put him over the edge. Ken wanted Michael to exit Dana's life, but that alone didn't seem a solid motive for murder. Ken also lost millions in a shady business deal brokered by Michael. Money was always a solid motive. He was alone in the house and had an emergency key that Dana gave him. Means, motive, and opportunity.

The final and most plausible explanation for Amy's death was that she was so drunk she fell over the cliff. It wasn't the first time someone died in that area from a misstep after using drugs or alcohol. Michael may have felt guilty for allowing it to happen.

But in Detective Connors' experience, he learned to trust his gut, and none of this felt right to him. The detective looked at the photos scattered across his desk. The scene in Michael's study looked staged and had a similar element to what they found on Amy's body at the base of the cliff. He and his team kept details of the investigation out of the press. Tracing its origin turned up nothing so far, but he needed to keep trying.

Ward Everly took a break from watching Susan DiMarco and walked into Hector's Hardware store to get duct tape.

"Hey, there, Ward," said Hector. "How's business?"

"Steady as always, knock on wood."

"Did you hear about the trespasser over at The Peabody Mansion?" asked Hector, as he rang up the purchase.

"Nope. What'd you hear?"

"Somebody, dressed all in black, was running around the woods over there. My buddy Ace ran after him and got him long enough to rip a piece of fabric from the guy. He's lucky Ace didn't take a chunk of leg with it." Hector chuckled at the thought. "The only thing that stopped him was Charlie Osgood yelling at him to come back."

"Who told you that?"

"Well, you know, word gets around."

Ward held his bag up. "Thanks, Hector."

"Be seeing ya."

Back at the truck, Ward sat for a few minutes chewing on the information Hector shared. What was going on over at the inn? With Dana there, she was at risk, and he couldn't have that.

He headed home and switched vehicles to drive back to the movie set. He wanted to see what Susan DiMarco was up to.

By the time he got there, it was lunchtime. He crept through the woods and found Susan eating alone, as usual. Tired of the games, he came out of hiding and approached her, making her jump.

"What's your problem?" she said, angry at being startled.

"You're my problem," Ward said, pointing a finger at her. "How does it feel to be targeted like you're targeting Dana?"

"I'm doing no such thing!"

"And what about the article they found on the trail? Where did that come from?"

"How should I know?"

Susan stood up to meet his gaze a foot shy of where his eyes looked down at her.

"I called my ex. She told me she interviewed with the La Jolla Hollywood News. That cheap tabloid that only reaches cities in SoCal. So how did it get here?"

Susan was quiet. Ward waited, glaring at her. She turned away.

"Who sent it to you?" he growled.

"My agent, Mel. He knows I'm interested in news about Amy Davis."

"Is it about Amy Davis or about me?"

"You threatened me at the party. I know you planted my witch's wand at the scene of the fake

murder."

"Just proving a point."

"And what point is that?"

"That you better watch yourself with Dana Wood. If anything happens to her, you're the first one they'll look at. I'll make sure of it."

"I was making a point, too, with the article."

"And what's that?"

"Everyone has secrets."

〰

Gail rang Dana to see how things were going. Dana didn't tell her about the new house, since Gail was famous for sharing good news before it was time.

"That prank we pulled at the party went national in the entertainment rags. Albert must be thrilled with the publicity," said Gail.

"Yes, and he had the best time doing it."

"I thought about you moving out there, and at first I was reluctant, but with Albert there, it's a smart move. Our joke proved that we can get you publicity no matter where you live."

Dana struggled not to tell Gail about her fabulous new house.

"It's going to be fantastic for me. There are lots of industry movers on the East Coast. Now we have another source of work and a chance to build relationships."

"That attitude is why you're a queen in this industry. If anything breaks, you'll be the first one I call."

〰

Susan wondered who the teenager was. She saw her at the Halloween Extravaganza talking to Dana, along with the young woman. Odd that the girl looked a little like Dana. The shape of her eyes and face were similar, but the skin tone was slightly lighter. Was the teen Dana's relative?

129

She kept her ears open for introductions rather than asking people about her. Her inquiry could spark suspicion, and the cast and crew protected Dana from nosey people.

Besides being shunned by those she worked with, now she had Ward Everly on her back, watching her every move. He snuck up on her in the woods. How long had he known about her secret lunch spot? She needed to take care around him. If he figured out that she'd planted the newspaper clipping, who knew what else he could discover.

ೞ

Zelda Weems came out of her stupor to find herself a block from Dana Wood's house in Beverly Hills, which was at least five miles from where she lived at Amy's in Los Angeles. She rubbed her temples and thought about Michael's death. The grapevine said he didn't commit suicide, that it was murder. If Zelda could get to Dana's house during a blackout, it wasn't out of the question to end up at the park where Amy died.

Her therapist suggested that Zelda had underlying resentment toward Amy and subconscious blame for her death. She had no reverence when going through Amy's things. They were just objects to sell and profit from. To be honest with herself, she rarely thought about Amy since the funeral. Walking through the house, it seemed Amy never lived there, her imprint missing from the rooms.

Zelda considered that Amy's shallow presence made the place seem devoid of her niece's energy. Her own drug dependence and dulled perception might be a contributing factor.

If the therapist was right, could Zelda have killed her niece and subsequently her lover? Did her anger and resentment run so deep as to wipe two people from the face of the earth? The ease of pushing someone over a cliff to their death seemed a good way to approach murder, unless the victim survived the fall. Zelda could have hit Amy with the bat she carried when walking alone, prompted by a documentary of a California serial killer lurking about, and then pushed her over.

She looked around. Her car was half a block away. It scared her to think she drove during one of her blackouts. Walking cleared her head, so she continued down the sidewalk until she stood in front of the gates of Dana Wood's driveway. A moving truck cautiously made its way between the gateposts, the driver looking both ways before moving onto the street.

Zelda looked down the driveway. The house hid behind bushes growing in the middle of the circular drive. Was it possible that she came here, got past the gate, and walked up the driveway to end Michael Williams' life? The prospect frightened her, yet she'd driven this far without knowing it. If there was no awareness of what she was doing, there was no fear.

The gates clicked shut as she walked back to her car.

ଔଓ

Autumn parked in the garage, turned off the alarm, and twisted her key to open the kitchen door. Chrissy bounced up the three steps and into the gourmet kitchen designed by Autumn's mother, Stella Clarke, and ran over to her empty cut glass bowls. She looked at Autumn, who filled her water bowl with fresh filtered water. Chrissy's took her time lapping up the water with her tiny tongue. Finished, she smiled up at Autumn, water dripping from her beard.

"Was that good, sweetheart?"

Chrissy wagged her tail and pawed at her empty food dish. Autumn poured a little kibble mix into the bowl. Chrissy ate slowly, chewing and savoring each bite while Autumn watched. She loved watching her little girl taking great pleasure in every mouthful. Chrissy drank a little more water and then walked away from her feeding station.

She waited patiently by the sliding door.

"Rediscovering your house, eh?" Autumn said as she pulled back the door.

Chrissy took off, running in circles in the grass. A squirrel caught her attention, and she chased it for a minute before losing it up a tree. Autumn protectively watched her. Despite the fenced yard, other potential dangers had squeezed under the barrier in the past, like skunks. Chrissy squatted and raced back to the house, leaping through the door and shaking out her lustrous hair. Her orange bow slipped, and Autumn re-clipped it to her pigtail.

"Good girl!"

Chrissy took off into the den, where her big toy pile awaited. Stuffed pigs, dogs, chipmunks, and some mystery creature covered in green fabric, in all shapes and sizes lay among squeaky toys, chew toys, balls, and holiday-themed toys. Chrissy dove under the round dog bed they sat on, pushed in, lifted it up, and tossed her toys all over the floor.

Autumn laughed.

"Are you having fun?"

Chrissy wagged her tail and batted her toys around.

131

It felt good to be home. Even though the mansion was so close, with all that was going on there, Autumn hadn't been home in weeks. She went out the front door to retrieve the mail. She tossed most of it after removing her name and address and kept bank statements and such. She had her bills on automatic payment, so bills never came to the house.

The redesigned upstairs master bedroom smelled of fresh paint and new furniture. Her heart fluttered thinking about sharing this room with Ray by Christmas. She transformed what used to be her parents' bedroom into a modern space that reflected her own taste. The closets were emptied and donated to a veteran's organization. Her clothes hung in what was her mother's closet. Her father's awaited Ray's clothes. She missed them every day, but knew they would have wanted her to move ahead with her life. They would have loved Ray and Ace.

She checked the other three bedrooms, one of which served as her office. Ray would get his pick of the other two as his personal space.

She heard the doorbell and went downstairs. Chrissy was already at the front door, wagging her tail and barking.

"Okay! Okay!"

Steve Coleman and Mickey stood on the front step.

"Come on in, guys."

Steve unclipped Mickey's leash so he could follow his friend into the den.

"Happy Monday!"

"How did you know I was here?"

"I saw you pull in from down the street."

"I don't have much to eat in the house, but I have tea and coffee."

"Coffee for me."

Steve sat at the kitchen table.

"Feels like old times."

"Oh, come on! I haven't been gone that long!"

"Seems like it. Mickey misses his morning walks with Chrissy."

"We'll be back soon, uh, here more often." Autumn didn't want to spill the beans about Dana moving out of the inn.

"You mean when Dana moves to that estate she bought?"

Autumn spun around and stared at Steve.

"How did you know?"

"Ran into Maureen Roberts at the grocery store."

"Wow, no keeping secrets in this town."

"What's the big deal?"

"After that shadowy intruder ran through the grounds, we wanted him to think Dana was still there so Ray, Ace, and Adam could catch him if he comes back."

"That plan's moot. Half the town probably knows about her living here permanently."

Autumn groaned.

After Steve and Mickey left, she called to tell Ray the secret was out, and they decided to stay in the mansion with Dana until the weekend, when she moved out on Sunday.

She updated Sarah Kelly about their needs through the end of the week, including two additional guests, being Stephanie and Adam. They would talk about a revised schedule once Autumn knew when she'd officially open.

Her goal was to make Dana's last week at the inn fun and relaxing.

Her next call was to Kim, who would be gone by the time Autumn and Chrissy arrived at the mansion. Business as usual through the end of the week, then a thorough cleaning of Dana's vacated room, followed by a special project in the attic with Kim, Elizabeth, Beatrice, and Autumn. Kim squealed and described a detailed plan of how she wanted to approach the work.

Exhausted from thinking about Kim's plan, she grabbed Chrissy and lay down on the couch, her arm drawing Chrissy's silky body close. They drifted off to sleep.

When Dana arrived back at the mansion that evening, Autumn told her that most folks knew about her home purchase.

"I should have asked Maureen to keep it quiet."

"Even if she had said nothing, the current owners might have let the news slip."

"I can tell my crew, then."

"I'd limit it to those closest to you and that's it. Those working on the film don't need to know just yet."

"You're right. We still don't know who was in the woods that night."

"To make you feel as safe as possible, we're adding Stephanie and Adam to our list of guests and testing out our new chef."

"It's comforting to know more eyes and ears are at the ready. As far as Chef Sarah, this kale, chickpea, and coconut curry dish is delicious." Dana dunked a piece of fresh-baked bread into the mixture.

"Looks like she passed the test. I'm not sure when I'll open the inn full time. I'm thinking after the wedding and Christmas, so I won't need her until January."

"I could use her until then, at least to make meals for me to pop into the microwave and when I entertain on weekends."

"Deal. Maybe we can share her after that."

❦

Gail was excited to hear about Dana's new house and vowed to make it back to Pennsylvania for Thanksgiving. Gail had nothing to report about the investigation, but tongues were wagging about Dana's sudden move. Part of the grapevine told a story that Dana worried about a killer running loose in California and that she might be next. The other part was that Dana made a major multi-movie deal with Albert Holton and the place to be for the best opportunities was on the East Coast. As long as they talked about Dana, Gail's work was done.

Ken Blanchard wasn't as cordial as Gail.

"You bought a house out there without talking to me about it first?"

"I appreciate your interest, Ken, but I don't have to get your permission."

"I'm here working my butt off to get you movie deals and you take off on me."

"What difference does it make where I live? I'm never home, anyway. I just got back from Scotland, remember?"

Ken was quiet for a few beats.

"You know, finding Michael was a shock. I guess I wouldn't live in a house where someone died."

"Then you better check the history of whatever house you buy in the area. There are lots of houses in L.A. with sordid histories that include death."

"I think the police are looking at me as a suspect. They don't think it was suicide. I heard they interrogated Zelda Weems, Amy Davis' aunt, too."

"I told them I asked you to check on Michael. And what would Zelda want with Michael?"

"The theory is she thought he killed Amy and wanted revenge."

"If he killed himself, I'm sad about that and wish he had gotten help. If someone murdered him, I want them to catch the killer. But other than finding the body, why would they look at you?"

Ken Blanchard cleared his throat.

"Michael dragged me into a scam business deal. I lost a few million."

"Why didn't you tell me?"

"It was between Michael and me. You were away at the time."

Dana thought for a moment.

"I need to work with people whose judgment I trust. I also want to trust those people to have my best interest at heart. Michael didn't, and his scam deal involved you without my knowledge."

"Dana, I, I… "

"I'm sorry, Ken. I need a fresh start. I wish you well. You'll get the commission from *Dark Hollow Road*, but as of today, I'm looking for new representation."

"I understand. I'm the one who needs to apologize," said Ken, his tone ashamed.

"Take care, Ken."

Dana tossed the phone on the sofa and lay across her bed, her arm over her eyes. Betrayal followed her wherever she went. What was it about the people she let into her circle? She guarded herself against most of the people in the industry. Her past was heavy with selfish people. Her own family made her give up her child for their own benefit. Her manager lied to her.

A piece was missing from her relationships with them. Intimacy. That's what was missing. The sense of closeness with someone who wants the best for you. Wants for you what you want for yourself and needs nothing in return.

That's the difference she felt here, with Autumn and Chrissy and all the rest. They put themselves at risk and made plans to keep her safe when there was nothing in it for them besides Dana's well-being. They treated their pets as part of the family, not accessories, as she'd seen pet owners in Hollywood do. She watched how much unconditional love passed between them. Even Maureen Robert's gossip about the house had no malice, just excitement about the sale and a new member of the community.

She vowed to use these people as a barometer for healthy relationships, especially Autumn and Chrissy.

The next morning, she asked Albert to join her in her trailer.

"Everything okay?"

"I have some news."

He waited.

"I bought a house in Knollwood! It's everything I've ever wanted."

"So we'll be neighbors. That's splendid news!"

"I'd like to keep it quiet for now. With the possible stalker at the mansion and Michael's death, I don't want any more news about me made public. Although, word spreads fast in this town."

"If the cast and crew find out, it won't come from me. Congratulations."

"I also fired my manager, Ken Blanchard. I'm looking for a new one."

"I have a couple names for you to check out."

Albert patted Dana on the shoulder.

"While you'll never be completely out of the spotlight, living here is more peaceful than in the rat race of L.A."

☙

Susan DiMarco couldn't wait any longer, so she took a chance and approached Dana as she left her trailer.

Startled, Dana said, "Hi, Susan. What can I do for you?"

"I'm wondering who your guests were, you know the young woman and the teenager."

"That's none of your concern."

"I saw them at the Halloween party. Who are they?" Susan pressed.

Dana didn't answer.

"The teenager looks familiar."

Dana's assistant ran over.

"We're ready for you, Dana."

Dana walked away without answering Susan's question, letting Susan know she'd struck a chord. There was something to this. Now it was a matter of learning more about this girl before going to the press.

☙

Dana felt a trickle of sweat run down her back. It was a mistake to invite Hannah to the set. She had similar features to Dana, making Susan question the resemblance.

Susan, of all people. No one else said anything. Susan was an entitled busybody who made Dana wary. That's all she needed was for Susan to leak suspicion to the press about Hannah. Investigative reporters had ways of finding out all kinds of things. She hoped it didn't come to that.

☙

Ward watched Susan approach Dana, whose face stayed calm until she turned away from Susan. Then her face turned tight with lips pressed together. What had Susan said to upset Dana?

136

Ward was on Susan before she could stop smirking. He grabbed the back of her costume so she couldn't run.

"What did you say to Dana?" he demanded.

"Nothing that concerns you."

"If it's about Dana, I want to know." He yanked her back when she tried to get away.

"Fine. I asked her about the visitors she had here. I saw them at the Halloween party and was just curious."

"Why is it any of your business?" Ward shook her.

"Exactly. Right back at you."

He wasn't getting anywhere.

"Remember, I'm watching you. Every move you make. Every person you talk to. I'll see."

"So what? I'm not doing anything illegal."

He pushed her away with a scowl.

"I can tell when someone's up to no good, and that's your game. It's for people who can't succeed on their own, so they try to take others down. It never turns out well for people like that. And you're one of those people."

Susan straightened her costume.

"Touch me again, and I'll have you thrown off the set."

She walked away, fists clenched.

Ward needed to find out what Susan was driving at in identifying the teenager. He knew the one she meant. The one with Kim. The one that looked like Dana. His gut tightened at the implication. He'd be watching.

⚡ **28** ⚡

Chrissy caused a stir on set. Cast and crew made a fuss over the darling little fuzz ball sporting pink ribbons in her pigtails. Pink was Chrissy's signature color, and Autumn was tired of seeing her in the seasonal orange and black bows.

Dana came over to them in full makeup so couldn't rub her face against Chrissy's, but she scratched Chrissy behind her ears.

"Thanks for inviting us, Dana."

"Glad you could make it."

Chrissy tugged at her leash.

"She has to go to the bathroom. Is there a good spot to take her?

"Those woods over there." Dana pointed to an area away from the activity.

"Be right back."

Chrissy stepped lightly over the leaves on the forest floor, sniffed, and squatted. She pulled Autumn deeper into the woods, looking and sniffing to find the perfect spot.

Leaves rustled to their right. Chrissy looked up and wagged her tail. She pulled Autumn closer to the sound. Ward Everly stepped out from behind a tree.

"Can't fool you, little one."

He reached in his pocket and broke off a piece of jerky. Chrissy reached out her tongue and gently took the snack, chewing it like it was a giant steak.

"She smelled the snack," Autumn said. "What are you doing out here?"

"Just taking a walk."

Autumn looked at him sideways. She wasn't buying his story but let it go.

"C'mon, sweetheart. Let's finish your walk."

She waved goodbye to Ward. Autumn felt his eyes on her, but didn't turn around.

Chrissy found her spot, and Autumn cleaned it up with a pink poo bag.

"Good girl! Let's go see Aunt Dana."

Chrissy trotted back toward the set, but stopped short. She stared through the trees and sniffed the air. Autumn followed her sightline and saw a woman dressed as a creature sitting beside a tree. The woman looked up and stared at them. Chrissy pulled Autumn closer, but it felt like an intrusion, so Autumn picked her up and walked back to the set.

Autumn saw a dumpster and stopped to dispose of the poo bag through a window on the side of the garbage bin. In Autumn's arms, Chrissy sniffed the air emanating from the garbage and barked.

"What is it? What do you see?"

Autumn stared at the trash, but didn't know what Chrissy reacted to. She put her head against Chrissy's. The image of black pants sticking out from under wrappers and other garbage hit Autumn's awareness. She called Ray and told him about Chrissy's find. He asked her to stay put until he got there.

Lieutenant Ray Reed, Ace, and officer Charlie Osgood met them at the dumpster and put cones and orange tape around it. They used a long-armed grabber-reacher tool to retrieve the pants from the dumpster. The fabric stretched as Charlie pulled it free of the surrounding garbage. Ace sniffed it and barked once, indicating he remembered those pants. Ray held open a large evidence bag and noticed a rip in the leg. Charlie lowered the garment into the bag, and Ray sealed it.

Their activity drew attention from the cast and crew, but no one approached them. Charlie left, heading to the lab with the evidence. Ray stayed behind. Without disrupting the production, he interviewed each member of the cast and crew in moments between performing their work.

The trash company positioned the dumpster behind the trailers to hide it from view, so most remembered using it themselves, but only two members of the film staff saw anyone approach the dumpster. They remembered Susan DiMarco offering to take trash from the set to throw it away for them. It stuck in their memory because that was unusual for her to offer to do something like that.

When it came time to interview Susan DiMarco herself, Ray was told she didn't feel well and had returned to her hotel.

Ray said goodbye to Autumn and Chrissy and headed over to Susan's hotel.

He recalled his interview with her at the Halloween Extravaganza, after being caught snooping around in Gail's room. Her attitude was defensive and annoyed. She came across as sneaky and manipulative, her answers short. While that was a minor infraction, here she was again.

Ray and Ace walked into the lobby and spotted Susan talking to the woman at the desk, still wearing her creature makeup.

"May we have a word?" Ray asked Susan.

"I'm busy right now."

"We can do this here or back at the station."

Susan reluctantly went to a private corner of the lobby, Ace on her heels.

"Get that dog away from me."

"He's here as a witness."

She pressed her lips together and wiped her hands on pants that made her legs look scaly.

"Do you recall the type of trash you disposed of in the dumpster recently?"

"Why would I remember that?"

"Some of your colleagues said you took their trash over to the bin. Said it was unusual for you to offer."

"So what? I'm trying to get them to like me."

"Did you toss anything else in the dumpster along with their trash?"

"I might have."

"Do you recall a pair of stretch pants being part of the trash you threw away for cast members?"

"Maybe."

"The people who mentioned your good deed wear a larger size than those pants. The tag said extra small. What size stretch pants do you wear?"

She hesitated. "Extra small. But that doesn't prove anything."

"No, but the lab will. And Ace confirmed they were the same pants worn by the intruder at The Peabody Mansion."

She glowered at Ace. He made a low growl that caused her to sit back.

"What if they are mine?"

"Trespassing and discharging a firearm on private property near an occupied residence for starters."

"It was not a firearm!"

She stopped, realizing her error.

"Then what was it?"

"Firecrackers."

"Set off among trees and without the property owner's permission."

"It was no big deal."

"If the property owner presses charges, it could mean jail time and fines."

"I was just trying to scare her, not hurt her."

"Who?"

"Dana Wood. I thought if I could scare her, she'd leave the area, and I'd get her role in the film"

"So you admit to stalking her to make her feel threatened."

"I want an attorney."

⚜

When Ward learned that they caught the intruder and it was Susan DiMarco, he contributed what he knew in a statement that indicated Susan harassed Dana Wood on the movie set. The information was added to her file, but they couldn't hold her. When she returned to work, he stood guard, unseen and ever vigilant.

⚜

Folks on set treated her with caution, shunning her from their conversations. Albert Holton instructed her to stay away from Dana Wood. They continued to shoot her scenes, but banned Susan from having any scenes with Dana.

Mel Argento called her after he got word from the casting director.

"What were you thinking?!" Mel yelled into the phone. "Don't you have enough interpersonal issues on this production?"

"I thought you'd be happy if Dana got scared off, and I got her role."

"Are you delusional? Even if Dana left the film, you're the last person they'd consider to replace her."

"You don't know that for sure."

"Actually, I do. Word is out on the street. Your reputation is trash at this point. No one will hire you after this. Don't you get it?" said Mel, disbelief in his voice.

"What if I could prove that Dana Wood has a secret to hide and went to the press?"

"Stay away from Dana. Don't do anything that has to do with her. People think you're a nut. No reputable journalist would listen to you."

"But... "

"But, nothing. You have no credibility. Back off. Now. This is your final warning."

He hung up. Her plan had blown up in her face.

⚜

Dana did her best to focus on bringing her character to life, pushing away worries about Susan DiMarco's warped attempts to take Dana's place and the potential of her digging into Hannah's resemblance to Dana.

The crew applauded after most of her scenes, giving her confirmation that she successfully detached from her troubles. Her sense of safety was enhanced by knowing everyone on set kept a sharp eye on Susan. A security guard was posted at her trailer to prevent Susan from approaching or entering Dana's private space.

Dana sat in a director's chair with her name on it. She liked resting among the crew between scenes and watching how scenes were shot. The fall air was crisp. The backdrop of stunning red, orange, and yellow leaves lent magic to the atmosphere and lifted everyone's creativity and imagination.

A large tote bag sat on the ground near her chair. They were between scenes when a familiar ringtone wafted through the air. A generic version of the song "I Only Have Eyes for You," played from the depths of the bag.

It was Dana and Michael's wedding song. When he found a version of it for his ringtone, he purchased it and never changed it. He was the only person she knew who used it.

"Whose bag is this?" she asked of those standing near her.

"I think it's Susan's," somebody answered.

Dana called Lieutenant Ray Reed and reported her experience.

"You were right not to go in the bag. I'll contact your security on set and get them to secure the bag. Sit tight, Dana. I'm on my way."

Moments later, Dana's senior security guard came over and grabbed the strap using a gloved hand. Susan came running over.

"Hey, that's my bag!"

"Yes, ma'am," said the guard.

"Give it to me!"

"I'm sorry. This is evidence."

"You don't have the right!"

Dana moved away from the fray, not wanting to get hit by Susan's flailing arms.

The other security guard came over and led Susan away from the area. She went kicking and screaming.

Ray finally arrived with Ace and a search warrant and confiscated the bag. He showed the warrant to Susan.

"Keep her here, please. Do you want to call your lawyer?"

"My phone is in the bag."

"May she use your phone?" Ray asked the security guard, who handed Susan his phone.

"I need my stuff!"

"You'll get back what belongs to you after we search the bag."

He walked toward Dana holding the tote bag.

"I need someplace to go through this privately."

"My trailer is right over there," Dana said, giving him the key. "Want to hold Ace?"

Dana gave a wan smile and took the leash. Ace sat upright next to Dana's chair and let her pet him.

Ray disappeared inside the trailer with a security guard to serve as a witness.

A half hour later, they emerged with a cell phone in a plastic evidence bag in one hand and Susan's tote in the other.

A uniformed officer arrived on the scene, and Ray instructed to take Susan into custody. They handcuffed her and loaded her into the back seat.

"Susan DiMarco, you're being arrested on suspicion of murder," said the officer. She was silent during the reading of her Miranda rights.

"Was it Michael's phone?" asked Dana, her voice quiet.

Ray nodded.

"I found the text she sent to you from his phone to establish her alibi. She was already in Pennsylvania when you received it."

"So, he didn't kill himself," Dana let out a deep sigh. "I'll let his mother know."

"Doesn't look that way. Detective Connors in L.A. realized they hadn't recovered Michael's cell phone at the scene, so he called it. That's when you heard the ringtone."

Dana shook her head.

"Should I be worried about her getting out?"

"If she does, we'll double the security on you. I'll let you hold onto Ace for the rest of the day if you want."

"I feel safer with him around. Thanks."

☙❧

Ward Everly watched the entire scene cloaked in the shadows of the trees. Susan was in custody, but with an attorney, she might get out on bail. He got in his car and drove into town, positioning himself across the street from the New Hope police station and jail on New Street. He pulled a sandwich out of his roomy pocket and munched. He'd stay for as long as it took.

⊗

Susan's lawyer arrived. They took him to the interrogation room where he sat next to her at the table. The room had television monitors, cameras, and recording equipment set up. A one-way mirror reflected Susan and her attorney sitting at the table. The lawyer opened his briefcase and took out a pad and pen.

"Ms. DiMarco, the charges filed against you are serious. Is there anything you can tell me before Lieutenant Reed and Detective Saunders arrive?"

"I stole Michael Williams' phone. So what?"

"Is that all I need to know?"

"Yes," said Susan, folding her arms in a huff.

"Do you want to talk to the police?"

"I don't care anymore," said Susan.

"Fine." The attorney got up and knocked on the door, letting them know he and his client were ready.

Ray Reed of the Knollwood police and New Hope detective Cartwright entered the room. Cartwright clicked the remote, bringing up Detective Connors of the Los Angeles police department on the screen. They all introduced themselves and advised that the session was being recorded.

"How did you happen to be in possession of Michael Williams' phone, Ms. DiMarco?"

"I took it from his study."

"When was that exactly?"

"Before I left to come here."

"Was Mr. Williams alive when you acquired the phone?" asked Detective Connors.

"You don't have to answer that," her attorney warned.

She didn't.

"How did you enter Mr. Williams' residence?"

"He let me in."

"So, you had a prior relationship with him?"

"You don't have to answer that."

"What was your relationship to the deceased? What brought you to his home?"

"We had no relationship. He broke it off. He kept me a secret. He ignored me!" Susan screeched, lifting herself off the chair.

144

Her attorney put a hand on her shoulder, but she pushed it away.

"Don't say anything else," he cautioned.

"It's all Michael's fault. And him with that floozy, Amy Davis. Flaunting her around town, while I got no publicity whatsoever!" Susan yelled, her face red from exertion and anger.

"Calm down. Let's take a break," the lawyer requested, but Susan kept going.

"What about Amy Davis?" asked Ray.

"She took him from me! She used him. They were in the park. I saw them out in the open all over each other. How dare they!"

The attorney moved his chair back, unable to steady his client.

"What did you do after you saw them together?" asked Detective Connors.

"I hit Michael with a rock and knocked him out. Amy saw me and started running. I caught her and used the rock to stun her, then pushed her over the cliff. She deserved it! Anyone in my position would do the same thing."

"Now you have Michael all to yourself," prompted Detective Cartwright.

"He wanted nothing to do with me! He said Dana still had his heart and he wanted to make it right with her. She was divorcing him! He should have been mine!" Susan sobbed. "Mine!"

"So, then what happened?" Detective Connors asked.

"I tried to kiss Michael in his study, he pushed me away. There was a statue on his bookcase, and I hit him with it. He went down. I think he died then, but it needed to look like suicide."

"I must strenuously advise you to stop talking, Ms. DiMarco," the attorney begged.

But Susan was in another world reliving the moment.

"He had a gun in his desk. He told me he kept it there in case a disgruntled investor confronted him. I put it in his hand and pulled the trigger."

"What about the note we found?"

"I wrote that. I knew the situation and made it sound like he wrote it."

"What about the text to Dana Wood?"

"That was part alibi and partly to make her suffer. This was her fault. All her fault!" Susan's face contorted in anger.

"I'd like to consult a physician to sedate my client."

"No! Get away from me!" she screamed and ran for the door.

She was quick, just like Charlie Osgood told Ray the night he chased her through the woods, and got past the officers in the hallway. Susan ran past the front desk and out into the street.

Ward saw her blast out of the police station door and charge down the street toward the Delaware River. He ran after her.

Moments later, Ray and the others came crashing through the doors. One jumped in a car, and Ray followed on foot. He saw Ward running up ahead and cursed under his breath.

Susan charged down the road toward the bridge near the Bucks County Playhouse. On the bridge, she turned to look behind her and tripped, hitting the wall and catapulting over it into the rocks and water below.

Ward watched her go over, as did Ray from farther away. Onlookers screamed as Susan tumbled into the water, cracking her head on the rocks. Ward bent over the side and saw her body floating right before it went over the falls. Ray skidded to a stop and saw Susan's lifeless body float away into the river current.

⚡ **29** ⚡

The entertainment news media and social media exploded with the story of Susan DiMarco murdering Michael Williams and Amy Davis. A few crew members anonymously added to the story by revealing Susan's strange behavior and harassment of Dana Wood. Her name starred in headlines connected to the three famous names she'd envied. Susan was right that death was the path to her fame.

The Knollwood Gazette splashed the news across the front page, touting Lieutenant Ray Reed and Ace as local heroes. The paper featured their photo under the headline. The reporter described Susan DiMarco's death as a tragedy waiting to happen and interviewed several people from *Dark Hollow Road* about their distrust and caution around her.

Farther down the page, news of their new town resident, Dana Wood, was a welcome addition to their community, and described her generous support of the animal shelter. It also asked residents to treat Dana Wood as a neighbor, not a Hollywood star, and to make her feel comfortable.

 number ♋

Detective Connors searched Susan's small apartment. There were no personal photos. The drab colors in the one-bedroom space held no joy. A decorative pillow sat centered on the bed with the message *Wake me up when I'm FAMOUS.*

Piles of binders sat on the floor, filled with newspaper and magazine clippings about actors and Hollywood industry deaths. After some research, he found that Susan was listed as a cast member in at least ten of the productions where a death occurred among those associated with the film. The files listed some victims as accidental or suicide. Some cases remained open and unsolved. He considered Susan DiMarco as the missing link in all ten of those deaths, knowing that Amy Davis was initially listed as accidental and Michael Williams was first thought to be a suicide.

He flipped through bundles of handwritten journals organized by date. Raging, hateful words filled their pages. The intensity reminded him of Susan's outburst during questioning. Connors planned to check the entries against the deaths in the binders to see if any confessions turned up.

He wrote an email to Lieutenant Reed and Detective Cartwright sharing the update of his valuable find. Their help, and maybe fate itself, were essential to bring this criminal to justice.

☙

Zelda Weems sighed with relief after reading about Susan's confession. It made her assess her state of being, walking around in a fog, and unsure of her actions. She threw away her medications and sold Amy's house. Most of the home's contents had sold to locals and online, so Zelda was flush with cash. She looked up small towns in New Mexico and purchased a modest house on five wooded acres with money to spare. She hoped to find a good therapist and get a fresh start. Maybe she would paint abstract flowers like she used to and sell her art at festivals. Shedding the old life and her peculiar reputation gave her freedom and hope for the future.

☙

The Gazette story didn't mention Ward Everly, but he didn't mind. His role had always been behind the scenes and in the shadows. Having Dana close by gave him opportunities to safeguard her when she was in town, the way he watched his neighbors and customers.

He did the same thing while living in La Jolla and eventually moved because some found his guardianship creepy. Ward's purpose was to keep away evil. The only way to do that was hiding in the shadows, where wrongdoers overlooked him.

Ward sensed that Chrissy understood his intentions. She had her own instincts about people. Ace, too, the way he went after Susan in the woods. He knew she was up to no good. Animals are smart that way.

Lieutenant Reed prohibited Ward from participating in police business, so he would keep to the edges of Knollwood. Lots went on in this small town without being reported to the authorities. He could intervene before the intended victim knew they were in danger. He has lots of practice in the Navy and studied stealth techniques intended to surprise the would-be criminal.

Susan DiMarco's death kept her from revealing whatever she thought about Dana Wood's connection to Hannah Stokes. Just because there was a resemblance meant nothing. He made a silent vow

148

never to mention it and to block nonsense rumors if he heard any. So far, he hadn't.

He liked Knollwood, so planned to stay out of Ray Reed's way. Residents used him because of Ward's expansive and surprising skill set, his reputation for completing the work on time and on budget, and because they felt safe around him. Ward had plenty of work to keep the money flowing. Autumn had already booked him for next year's maze building, probably on the advice of Chrissy the wonder dog.

ଓଞ୍ଚ

Gail flipped the pages in awe, getting shivers as she read about Susan DiMarco's role in the deaths. How had she been so clueless? To think Susan had been in her room. Since then, Gail inspected everything she brought back with her to make sure Susan hadn't poisoned her or harmed her things. She looked at those around her with suspicion, not trusting like she used to.

Susan's unexpected death put Gail at ease for Dana's safety. She looked forward to spending a long weekend at Dana's new estate for Thanksgiving. She'd drum up business from the East Coast actors and from Albert Holton. He respected her opinion on garnering publicity after their Halloween stunt created buzz for his film from coast to coast.

Gail looked forward to being bi-coastal and thought about contacting Maureen Roberts to find her an idyllic Bucks County home to work from.

ଓଞ୍ଚ

The experience Elizabeth gained on-set was a dream come true. Her skills were still in demand with her current clients and gained others when they found out she worked with Albert Holton and Dana Wood. With the dramatic increase in work, Elizabeth hired an assistant smart enough to be her office manager and strong enough to help her lift and move heavy decorative elements. Kim Stokes also volunteered to help when she could.

Dana Wood turned out to be an unanticipated mentor who recognized Elizabeth's talent and put her in a position to show people what she was capable of. The woman cared about people, and Elizabeth liked and respected her.

Autumn also gave her opportunities and artistic freedom to showcase Elizabeth's gifts to the public. She had a complete vision for Autumn and Ray's wedding, with some surprise elements they would

149

love. She'd make the mansion a winter fantasy land and decorate a soaring artificial tree. Autumn warned her about cutting down a tree for this purpose. It was either get one to replant, root ball and all, or use an artificial tree they could use for years to come. Elizabeth figured they could store the artificial tree in the attic, so planned on that.

Working at the mansion felt like working with good friends who wanted the best for you. Working on set was like going back to school with caring professors ready to teach you the ropes. Elizabeth Johnson considered herself blessed.

☙❧

Kim Stokes thought about how close she'd been to a real-life killer. Chills ran down her back. She shook them off and turned her mind to Dana Wood, thanking goodness that Dana was safe. She looked forward to Thanksgiving with her family, where Kim and Hannah would share their adventures with Dana Wood and her generosity, along with their hope that she'd keep giving them free movie tickets.

Kim loved working with Elizabeth, both at Autumn's and on Elizabeth's other jobs. The attic was a treasure trove and ripe for organization, which was Kim's favorite activity. Autumn gave her a vase and antique tea set Kim admired.

The day that Stacey Eldridge and Clay came over to value the books was especially fun, hearing Stacey squeal with each rare volume she discovered.

One day, Autumn made tea and snacks. They sat together in the living room with Chrissy, and Autumn sprung an idea she never thought would come. Autumn asked if she was interested in becoming assistant manager for The Peabody Mansion B&B. For the time being, the duties still included cleaning, but also maintaining the website with events, specials, and marketing the inn's opening when the time came. Kim would also welcome guests and handle the front desk. The promotion came with a bump in pay.

The raise plus the work with Kim put her in a great financial position, and she could buy her family the best Christmas presents ever.

Autumn woke up in her own bed and smiled at her sweet-faced Shih Tzu. She pulled Chrissy closer. Autumn loved snuggling her, especially after last night's bath made her hair smell fresh. She kissed Chrissy's head and heard her grunt.

Pulling on a robe, she lifted Chrissy off the bed and downstairs. The moment the sliding door opened, Chrissy walked onto her patio and smelled the air before continuing onto the grass. Autumn stood outside watching her fur baby and marveling at how her unique gift had helped catch Susan DiMarco. She was grateful that they could protect their new friend, Dana Wood, from Susan's desperation.

It saddened Autumn to think of the emotional and mental pain Susan must have been in to commit her crimes and hoped she was now at peace.

Halloween was lively, with lots of kids coming to the door and Chrissy greeting each one in her butterfly costume. The children loved it and got a thrill from the full-sized candy bars Autumn gave out.

With November finally here, the leaves grew darker and fell from the trees, creating big piles for Chrissy to play in before the landscapers hauled them away.

Life returned to its normal pace: morning walks with Steve and Mickey, afternoon naps with her silky pup, and evenings snuggling in front of the fireplace with Ray and Ace.

Autumn was so proud of Ray and his promotion. His excitement and dedication to his new role lifted her heart and brought joy to their little family.

The means to create happiness for others brought the greatest joy she'd ever known. From helping the animal shelter, to giving opportunities to others, allowing them to grow and prosper, her life fulfilled her. Autumn planned to follow in her mother's footsteps and find more ways to help the community.

Chrissy trotted into the house and got a drink of water.

"Do you know how much I love you?" Autumn said to Chrissy.

Chrissy looked adoringly at Autumn, ran past her, and grabbed her favorite piggy toy, bowing down to challenge Autumn, tail wagging. Autumn grabbed the toy and threw it across the den. Chrissy hopped after it and shook it until Autumn came to pull it from her mouth and throw it again.

⅋

The weekends leading up to Thanksgiving gave Dana a chance to get settled in her new home and prepare the guest quarters for Gail. She roamed the grounds and sat by the pond, thinking about Susan DiMarco and the trouble she'd brought to so many lives.

Michael's mother, relieved to hear he had not taken his own life, expressed horror that someone had the gall to take her son's life from him. Upon hearing of Susan's demise, his mother remarked, "Serves her right."

She felt safe in the house and in Knollwood. The article about her in the Knollwood Gazette and the reporter's plea to citizens to let Dana have privacy and a normal life here delighted her. Her stress came down a few notches knowing she was part of a community that cared about her as a person, not a commodity.

Dana's first Thanksgiving in her new house was a grand affair. The table had room for a dozen guests, and Dana filled each chair. Albert Holton and his wife, Mia, Gail Armstrong, Autumn and Ray, Stephanie and Adam, Beatrice and Jasper, and Steve and Lisa Coleman. Chrissy, Ace, and Mickey had their own eating area a few feet away, the floor laid with placemats, china, and crystal for their canine dinner feast and treats throughout the day.

She thought of Hannah and wondered if she really was the daughter she had given up so long ago. Dana knew it was best to let Hannah live her life and pictured her enjoying the holiday with her family. She'd continue giving movie tickets to Kim and Hannah, but decided not to take the chance of standing next to Hannah. She didn't want people having thoughts in a direction that might dig up the past.

Dana hadn't cooked in ages. It was fun creating a traditional Thanksgiving meal. Autumn, Lisa, and Dana did most of the cooking. Gail, Mia, and Stephanie drank most of the wine, and the men downed scotch and beer while watching football in the den, yelling at the action on the big screen. Those who didn't cook, bought, and their contributions loaded the buffet counter with pumpkin pie, apple pie, chocolate fudge cake, and chocolate chunk cookies.

Dana watched Chrissy make the rounds in between play sessions with her friends, ensuring everyone had a chance to make a fuss over her beauty and show her some affection.

152

Wine flowed, and laughter filled the air. Dana's dearest dreams were now a reality, with a home filled with friends, love, and gratitude on this special holiday and every day.

Book Club Questions

1. Do you feel pity for Susan when she showed her full unbalanced mind at the end, or do you think Susan was trying to show everyone her acting skill?

2. Do you believe dogs (or any pet) can bring psychic energy, such as healing or strength, to a stranger similar to Chrissy and Dana's early interactions?

3. Do you think Dana will approach Hanna about the true nature of their relationship? Why or why not?

4. Autumn and Ray have pushed up their wedding date. Do you think this is a sign of Autumn's complete psychological healing?

5. What do you think about Autumn's generous and loving commitment to Beatrice's well-being? Does it seem like genuine affection and friendship, or the result of a guilty conscience?

6. How do you feel about Dana's decision not to reveal her true identity to her daughter, Hannah? If you were in Dana's situation, what would you do?

7. Do you think adopted children have the right to know who their birth parents are?

8. If Dana finally meets Hannah's adoptive parents, should she reveal her true identity to them?

9. What are some difficulties Dana may face going forward if she chooses not to reveal her identity?

10. When did you realize who the killer was? When did you first suspect him/her?

11. Did Susan's narcissistic and sociopathic behavior remind you of anyone in your life?

12. How did Ward's obsession with Dana start? How long had he had been stalking her before his first letter? Did you think he was a danger to her? Do you think they could begin a more normal relationship now that Dana has moved to Knollwood, or is Ward's fixation too overwhelming for Dana to tolerate?

13. What do you think about Ray refusing to move in to the mansion before the wedding? Do you think that is still a meaningful gesture in this day and age?

14. What did you think about the Halloween Extravaganza at the mansion? Would you want to attend the party? Would you ever host an event like that at your own home?

Scavenger Hunt Checklist

Use this list on Halloween night and see how many you can spot!

Check	Item	Check	Item
	Gargoyle		Witch
	Scarecrow		Vampire
	Corn Stalks		Ghost
	Skeleton		Grave Marker
	Dog in a Costume		Cat in a Costume
	Carved Pumpkin		Uncarved Pumpkin
	Orange Twinkle Lights		Candy Corn

Fall Recipes from Lisa Coleman's Kitchen

All recipes created by:
Chef Jacquie Peccina-Kelly
www.strEATSofPhillyFoodTours.com
610-506-6120

Stuffed Mushroom Caps ala Chrissy*

[*Please note this recipe is named after Chrissy, but is **NOT** for dogs, as it contains garlic and walnuts, which can be toxic to pets]

INGREDIENTS:

- 8-ounce package of white button or cremini mushrooms
- 1/3 cup fresh Italian Flat Leaf Parsley, roughly chopped
- 1/3 cup walnuts
- 2 large cloves of garlic, roughly cut
- ½ teaspoon Kosher Salt
- 3 Tablespoons of Extra Virgin Olive Oil (I use Cardena's Organic Tunisian EVOO) https://cardenastaproom.com/
- ½ cup of panko breadcrumbs
- ¼ cup grated Parmigiano Reggiano cheese

Prep mushrooms:
Gently clean mushrooms with a damp paper or cloth towel.

Remove stems and gills and set aside. I peel off the thin outer layer of the mushrooms and set the scraps aside with stems and gills. My secret weapon for removing mushroom gills is the small handle of a demi (espresso) spoon, fork, or iced tea spoon.

Add parsley, garlic, walnuts, oil, and salt, half of the grated cheese and mushroom scraps, gills and stems to a food processor. Pulse until all is well combined and walnuts are little chunks.

Place in a bowl and add panko bread crumbs and stir until all is incorporated.

Spoon mixture into mushroom caps and then place them onto the aluminum lined cookie sheet and put in the refrigerator for 30 minutes.

Preheat oven to 400 degrees.

Drizzle mushrooms with extra virgin olive oil and top with rest of grated cheese. Place cookie sheet in oven to cook for about 25-30 minutes or until cheese is golden brown.

Kale and Chickpea Curry with Jasmine Rice

How to make perfect rice every time:
- 1 cup Jasmine or other white rice

- 2 cups water

- ½ teaspoon kosher salt

In a medium sized saucepot, over high heat, add all ingredients and stir.

Bring to a boil, stir again and then turn heat to low.

Cover pot with lid and cook for 20 minutes.

Do not touch the lid for 20 minutes! Remove pot from stove and fluff rice with a fork and then set aside.

INGREDIENTS:
- 3 Tablespoon of your favorite curry spice (I love the Spice House Brand of French Masala Curry)

- 14-ounce can of coconut milk

- 15-ounce can of chick peas, drained and rinsed

- 1 bunch of kale, stems removed, roughly chopped and cleaned (prepackaged has a lot of stems)

- ½ medium onion, chopped

- 2 cloves of garlic, minced

- 1 cup of whole San Marzano peeled tomatoes with juice, chopped

- 2 teaspoons Kosher salt

- 2 tablespoons extra virgin olive oil

In a medium deep-frying pan, over medium/high heat, sauté onions for 4 minutes, until translucent.

Add garlic, salt and curry spice, cook another minute.

Add kale and sauté for 3 minutes, then add tomatoes and coconut milk, bring to a boil, then turn heat down to low and simmer for 15 minutes.

Serve over a scoop of Jasmine rice or firmly pack rice into a small ramekin and place in the middle of a bowl and then ladle curry into bowl.

Whipped Butternut Squash – 2 Ways

INGREDIENTS:
- 1 butternut squash
- 1 Tablespoon of extra virgin olive oil
- ½ teaspoon salt
- 1/8 teaspoon of fresh ground pepper
- 2 Tablespoons of butter
- 1-2 Tablespoons of dark brown sugar
- Salt Flakes, fresh ground black pepper and brown sugar for garnish

Prep squash for roasting:

Preheat oven to 350 degrees.

Trim off top of squash and cut squash in half, lengthwise. Place on an aluminum lined cookie sheet, cut side up.

Drizzle with oil and sprinkle with a few pinches of salt and pepper and place in oven. Roast for about 45 minutes to an hour. To check for doneness, insert a fork all the way through effortlessly.

Remove from oven and let squash cool.

Scoop out squash and place in a bowl with butter, rest of salt and pepper, and whip with an electric beater, on high speed, until well combined.

Place mixture in sauce pot and warm through and then divide squash mixture into 2 separate serving bowls.

1st bowl – savory – adjust seasoning, salt, pepper and butter and stir. Before serving, top with a small pinch of salt flakes and fresh ground pepper.

2nd bowl – sweet – adjust seasoning, salt, pepper, butter, add brown sugar, and stir. Before serving, top with a small pinch of brown sugar, salt flakes, and fresh ground pepper.

Pumpkin Ravioli

INGREDIENTS:

- 1 dozen Talluto's pumpkin ravioli
- 1 stick of salted butter
- 10-12 fresh sage leaves
- Freshly grated Parmigiano Reggiano cheese

Cook the ravioli according to the package.

In a small frying pan, over medium heat, add the stick of butter.

When butter has melted and starts turning brown, lower to a simmer and add fresh sage leaves; cook 1-2 minutes.

Drain ravioli and place on a serving platter.

Drizzle with brown butter and add as much freshly grated Parmigiano Reggiano cheese as you desire.

A few options: use regular butter sauce instead of brown butter. Pumpkin gnocchi or butternut squash filled ravioli are great alternatives. Add crumbled Amaretti cookies on top of the ravioli for a little bitterness and an unexpected crunch for a rich, autumn flavor.

This recipe is so easy to make, you can have pumpkin ravioli in a snap.

Autumn's Fall Salad

This is the perfect salad for autumn and holiday dinners. I combine butter lettuces, fresh spinach leaves, diced apples, cranapple vinaigrette and crumbled Bleu cheese to top it off.

Cranapple Vinaigrette

INGREDIENTS for Cranapple Syrup:

- Quart of apple cider
- 1 cup fresh cranberries
- ¾ cup sugar
- 1/8 cup chopped shallots

INGREDIENTS for Vinaigrette:

- 1-1/2 ounces apple cider vinegar
- 3 ounces extra virgin olive oil
- 4 ounces Cranapple syrup
- Salt and pepper to taste

DIRECTIONS for Cranapple Syrup:

Combine all ingredients in saucepan.
Bring to a boil and then turn the heat down to a simmer.
Reduce until a syrup consistency is achieved.

DIRECTIONS for Vinaigrette:

In a self-contained jar/bowl add all ingredients.
Shake vigorously.
Cover and refrigerate until ready to use.

Linguini with White Clam Sauce

INGREDIENTS:
- 1 pound linguini
- 1 bag of little neck clams
- 3 medium cloves of garlic, finely chopped
- 1 Tablespoon of flat leaf parsley, finely chopped
- 1/3 cup dry white wine (I use Francis Ford Coppola Winery Chardonnay) *link
- ½ cup seafood stock or clam juice
- 1 - 6.5 ounce can or jar of chopped clams. Reserve the 1/3 cup of clam juice
- 1/3 cup of extra virgin olive oil
- ¼ teaspoon crushed red pepper chili flakes
- Juice from ½ lemon
- 1/8 teaspoon of fresh ground black pepper

Prepping clams takes a little time. Place clams in a sink with cold water, don't cover clams with water. This helps with the clams letting out sand. I scrub every single one, I don't know anyone who likes sandy clams. I use a small hand brush.

Prepare linguini according to package directions and undercook them about 1-2 minutes.

In a large frying pan, over medium/high heat, sauté garlic, pepper and chili flakes for about 2 minutes. Add white wine and cook until evaporated. Add clam juice, seafood stock, parsley and lemon juice and bring to a boil. Add chopped and whole clams, stir and cover pan with lid. Cook for about 5 minutes or until clams open. (Discard unopened clams)

Drain pasta, and add 1/3 cup of pasta water to the clam sauce, bring to a boil.

Add linguini to pan with sauce, toss and cook for 1 minute. Place pasta into a platter and garnish with clams and freshly chopped parsley.

About Chef Jacquie: Chef Jacquie is committed to sharing her culinary knowledge and expertise so that people who enjoy food can take their senses to new heights by simply tasting food around Philadelphia. She is the owner of strEATSofPhilly food tours and is a graduate of The Restaurant School. Founded in 1974 as The Restaurant School, Walnut Hill College is one of Philadelphia's first colleges to focus on excellence in hospitality education.

About the Author

Diane Wing, M.A. is a multi-published author of dark fantasy fiction, cozy mysteries, and enlightening non-fiction. Her work helps people see the magickal, spiritual, loving side of life with a practical edge. She grew up in a household where her vivid imagination could thrive. Crafting short stories and poetry from an early age, writing remained part of her life throughout her 25-year corporate career. Her training in clinical psychology shows up in her characters' struggles and in her non-fiction books about energetic consciousness, tarot, and happiness. Diane seeks to help the reader find the flame of their own unique life path sparked by her stories and insights for personal growth. Diane is an avid reader, bibliophile, lover of trees and animals, and a lifelong learner. Connect with her and find out more at:

www.DianeWingAuthor.com

www.DianeWing.com

The Adventures of Autumn and Chrissy Begin Here

Only Chrissy, a cute little Shih Tzu, can unlock this mystery! Autumn Clarke survived the car crash that killed her parents. To help her cope with PTSD, she adopts Chrissy, a Shih Tzu with a remarkable secret. Chrissy is also the only witness to the mysterious death of her pet parent. Autumn vows to find the truth behind his death with the help of Chrissy, the neighbors and an attractive detective. Can Autumn unravel the clues while trying to heal Chrissy's trauma and overcome her own devastating emotional wounds in the midst of a dangerous murder investigation?

"Chrissy the Shih Tzu may be the cutest sleuth on the job, but don't let that button nose fool you—it's perfectly able to sniff out a killer with a little help from her human friends. Great start to a fun new series!"
—Sheila Webster Boneham, Author of the award-winning *Animals in Focus Mysteries*

"Diane Wing does an excellent job of showing readers just how animals can communicate with us through images and actions when we are tuned into their frequency. Through the relationship between Autumn and Chrissy, Wing also shows the importance of therapy animals and how much they can help those who need them. Add in a sweet romance to the intrigue of the mystery and you've got a book that you won't want to put down."
—Melissa Alvarez, Intuitive, animal communicator and author of *Animal Frequency* and Llewellyn's *Little Book of Spirit Animals*

"Diane Wing has created a wonderfully endearing little character in Chrissy the Shih Tzu. It really shines through that the author is an animal and dog lover. I can see these books quickly becoming a cherished addition to the cozy mystery genre."
—J. New, author of *The Yellow Cottage Vintage Mysteries*

Learn more at www.DianeWingAuthor.com

From Modern History Press

In this second installment in the series, Chrissy digs up clues to help Autumn solve a historical disappearance and a modern-day murder mystery

Autumn Clarke is getting her life back to normal with the help of her extraordinary shih tzu, Chrissy, when the death of a local philanthropist reveals the man's dark family secrets, as well as unexpected ties to Autumn. When Chrissy discovers a dog-eared diary in the dead man's family home, Autumn discovers that things in the Clarke family are not quite as they seem. Can Autumn interpret the hidden clues in the dog-eared diary to crack the most puzzling disappearance in Knollwood history? Are the recent murders connected to the past? Is Chrissy more insightful than Autumn realized?

"I have fallen in love with Chrissy and Autumn and their continuing journey to health while finding themselves in the middle of a murder mystery adventure. My pre-teen daughter and I enjoyed reading *The Dog-Eared Diary* and then discussing the clues, plot twists, and characters."

—Antoinette Brickhaus, Maryland

"Chrissy the Shih Tzu is a real character in the book and not just a prop to help the story along. Chrissy often felt like she was going to start talking. I loved the relationship between Autumn and her dog. The love the two of them have is absolutely perfect. Perfect for a rainy afternoon and one any cozy mystery fan will enjoy. I can't wait to see what happens next!"

—Andrea J. Guy

"I applaud the author for her use of so many clever writing devices within a rather brief cozy mystery. Nothing seemed contrived nor out-of-place. I hope that someone makes the decision to adapt these books to the screen because it would make one amazing mystery series!"

—Ruth A. Hill, journalist

Learn more at www.DianeWingAuthor.com

From Modern History Press